Alicia Albu

Rebecca Kelly

Adam Lyons

long story short

Hazel O'Sh

Niamh the
best 5th class
teacher, Stephen Tol

Rachael
Murray

Laura Rourke

Niamh,

Great teacher in
5th class Sarah
Aaron Page Moore

Tom knight
(Hold onto this it'll
be worth a bit in a few
years

Adam O'Rourke.

Dylan Forde

Matthew
Dolan. Niamh,
Best 5th class
teacher,
Alex O'Dea

Fighting Words is a creative writing centre, established by Roddy Doyle and Seán Love. It opened in January 2009 and aims to help students of all ages to develop their writing skills and to explore their love of writing.

www.fightingwords.ie

Donabate Community College is a co-educational second level school in County Dublin.

www.donabatecc.ie

long story short

Fourth Year Students,
Donabate Community College
Portrane Road, Donabate
Co. Dublin

Introduction by Paul Murray

FIGHTING WORDS
THE WRITE TO RIGHT

A Fighting Words Book

Long Story Short is published in May 2014 by Fighting Words

© Individual authors, 2014

Editor: Clara Phelan

Cover Design: Persuasion Republic

Printed by: Hudson Killeen, Blanchardstown, Dublin 15

Fighting Words
Behan Square
Russell Street
Dublin 1

www.fightingwords.ie

ISBN: 978-0-9568326-5-8

Fighting Words gratefully acknowledges funding support for its
publications from:

Contents

Introduction
Paul Murray

Why do we write? Why make any kind of art at all? There are many theories, but my favourite belongs to the German philosopher Friedrich Nietzsche. Art exists, he says unambiguously, to keep the truth from killing us. That's not to say we tell stories just to distract ourselves from what's really going on. Instead, writing is a way of gaining some measure of control on a reality that even on a good day can seem baffling and arbitrary. By telling stories about it, we find a place for ourselves in it, a space where we can breathe. And at the same time we can begin to make sense of our own feelings about ourselves and about being alive.

So even though stories by their nature are made up, to write them – to write good ones – requires a certain amount of exposure to the cold winds of truth. That's why the stories gathered here, written by transition year students at Donabate Community College, are so vivid and so fresh. While adult life, with its routines and repetitions, is something that all too many of us go through on autopilot, this is rarely the case with teenagers. The stakes tend to be a lot higher when you're fifteen or sixteen; the simplest events are fraught with meaning, sometimes (often) painfully so. I can still remember the crazy rollercoaster of emotion that constituted an ordinary school day, and I still have the reams of writing – stories, sketches, cartoons, poems – that those emotions produced. Very little would be what you could call art; but at the time it felt like it saved my life.

The stories in this collection are very different, exhilaratingly so. But they all share what you might call an unflinching quality, a determination to tell their own story their own way. The time spent developing their ideas at Fighting Words shows. In these pages you'll find madness, alienation, death; you'll find ghosts, thieves, murderous bingo players. You'll also find several representations of parents: be warned at the outset that many of them get killed off, and few of them come out looking particularly good. Take the terrifying Papa in Alicia Albu's 'Anger is a Killing Thing'. An inveterate racist, he sees a black fireman and tells his daughter, 'I'd run straight for the fire before he lay one of those dirty hands on me.' A doctor tells him that his rage does no one any good, least of all himself: 'Anger is a killing thing. It kills the man who lets it in, with each rage leaving him less than he had before'. But Papa doesn't listen, and ends up bringing down tragedy not only on himself but on his daughter. Alice's father in Sadhbh Mac Lochlainn's futuristic 'Foedus ad libertatem' is arguably even worse: 'Minister for Covert Affairs, possibly the most hated man on the planet right now.' When her mother is killed, Alice's whole belief system is turned on its head. 'The government were good and true and they saved us,' she tries to persuade herself. 'They brought us unity and peace and control. What the Foedus ad libertatem offered us was freedom and freedom led to chaos and chaos led to war.' But the Foedus ad libertatem, or League to Freedom, is her only hope of survival – along with her new friend Rebecca, whose trust and kindness enables Alice to find her fate in this turbulent new world.

Hazel O'Shea's eerie, gorgeously written 'Decay' is also set in the future, as Ellory and his unnamed sister explore a deserted settlement on an uninviting otherworld: 'Everywhere they looked was grey, as though the planet had been tipped over and all the colour drained out.' In this mysterious blankness the psychological traumas Ellory's sister has been hiding come alive: 'A child, wearing a uniform similar to her own, but with hair past her waist, stood to the right of her reflection. The girl had no features on her face, just smooth silvery white skin, and dark voids where eyes should have been. The familiar feeling of fear and euphoria chilled her bones. But she couldn't look away...'

The amplifying effects of loneliness and suffering are heartbreakingly rendered in 'Apartment Block 3' by Rebecca Kelly, where several sets of neighbours listen in on each other's lives while failing totally to understand them. Doris, trapped with an abusive, alcoholic husband, takes refuge in an old videotape of her wedding; in a neighbouring apartment, Dan, hearing the girl next door scream 'couldn't bring himself to care about what it was that she was so happy about.' Dan's a self-harmer, no less trapped than Doris: 'Every single time, it became harder and harder to feel something. Every single time, Dan had to go deeper.' But there is hope in the form of Matthew and Jamie, whose love for each other and sparky repartee enables them to overcome the violent intolerance they face.

More bad parenting is on view in Matthew Dolan's story, 'The Unexpected Hero', where Anna's mother and father spend their time bickering or drunk and never notice that their daughter has developed strange magical powers – although a family of vampires has taken a closer interest. Another Anna, also bad news for vampires, features in Rachael Murray's story, 'Life Beyond Pretty Flowers and Fairytales'. After killing a hellhound, Anna finds its owner, none other than the King of Hell, is on her trail.

Some of the stories get their energy from unusual narrative techniques. In Stephen Tol's 'Watching Richard', the boy's father narrates the story as a ghost, after his wife pushes him off a cliff. Alex O'Dea's 'Crash' uses a shifting perspective – from a drunk driver to his daughter to a weary paramedic – to show how one man's irresponsibility has consequences far beyond himself. Adam Lyons' cinematic 'Sweet Innocence' weaves different characters, from a bank worker to a bereaved mother to a just-released prisoner, into a tale that features a bank robbery, child kidnapping, and more than one Lamborghini. In 'Destroying my past' by Adam O'Rourke, John's discovery of his father's double-life is just the beginning of a story that thoroughly lives up to its title and conveys a genuine sense of anger: 'For 5 minutes they would be like "ahh bless him" or "the poor youngfella",' John thinks, leaving his foster home, 'then after the fake tears and the fake opinions they would laugh about the child who's so messed up that they looked after in their terrible excuse for a job.'

Clearly – unless there's something in the water in Donabate – all these wicked parents are meant metaphorically, standing in for the Truth Nietzsche talks about that will crush anyone who can't work out a strategy. In other stories, it takes on a more apocalyptic form. In Laura Bourke's 'The Road', some inept scientists accidentally unleash a horde of zombies, with whom Nicola soon finds herself acquainted: 'I turned around to see the rotting face of a middle-aged woman...It was almost like time had frozen...I stood still unable to move while her watering mouth inched closer and closer to me...' Sarah Moore's 'Underwater Ruins' is set in an underwater city on the brink of annihilation. Sarah and Martha's only chance is to make for the surface, which means losing everything they've ever known. Nevertheless, there's a sense they might be gaining something new: 'I looked over at Martha, her face was pressed against the window, she had never seen the surface or the sun. "So beautiful!" she whispered.'

It's not all apocalypse, however. One of the first stories I ever wrote was about a boy wooing a girl with bad poetry – which may or may not have been based on personal experience – so I was delighted to read Maeve Sweeney's hilarious 'A Poetic Fix', in which the narrator attempts to lassoo Shane O'Malley, 'hair as golden and luscious as a Crunchie', with verse. How could any man resist a poem like this?

Wow, can you see that moon?

Beautiful as any, like, tune,

So pretty and round,

I am, like, spellbound,

And this moment a sun would just ruin, like.

 Yet somehow you know Shane's not going to get it.

This is one of the few places love rears its head. Most of the stories' protagonists are loners. Some are that way by circumstance. The narrator of Dylan Forde's 'No Man's Land', for instance, is marooned on a desert island after his plane goes down. Tellingly, it's recovering his diary that keeps him sane: 'Now I know I'm not alone.'

Others, though, seek out isolation. Misanthropic van driver Dan, the central figure of Tom Knightly's story 'The Bingo Bus', can't even order a pint without threatening to break the barman's nose. Yet in elderly Mrs Macdunnagh he finds a kindred spirit – someone as bitter and misanthropic as he is. After hearing her extraordinary story he is moved to offer her his support: 'wha' I'm doing here is called helpin' ou' a fellow philosopher.'

Red Porter isn't stuck on an island, but he might as well be. The narrator of Ghail Protacio's witty 'Plan D' is a maddening, brilliantly realized archetype of teenage apathy: 'Every time they used to get us to imagine ourselves in "ten years from now" in school,' he tells us, 'I'd see nothing... I had no goals, no ambitions, and that was all I knew. I mean, I just turned eighteen last month, and I was already done with being eighteen.' Red's existential issues pale into insignificance, however, compared to what Trippy's going through in Luke Collins' exuberant graphic fiction, 'Trippy's Travels'. Hit by a plane, lost in a sewer, eaten by a shark? Although it's not impossible that at least some of this is happening in his imagination...

Whether under the influence or not, so many of these characters feel their place in reality to be precarious, and typically the way they tighten their grip is through some act of care, some extension of their thoughts beyond themselves. Sometimes this is on an epic level, as in Eoghan McGleenan's space opera 'Brothers Betrayed', in which twins separated at birth duke it out for the fate of the universe. Sometimes, as in Diane Pasague's poetic, moving story 'Forget Me, Forget Me Not', it's in remembering a lost friend. Nate takes refuge in an autumn meadow, and Leah, the little girl from the house next door, takes refuge in Nate. The meadow, 'drastically lonely', is a safe place their imaginations can unfold without the interference of the adult world; nature and memory, like art, provide ways to survive the brutal truth, if, in Leah's case, only temporarily.

It seems too late to help the title character of Aaron Page's 'The Man Who Lost His Spirit'. 'A long time ago he had lost a son; he had held him only once, and then had laid him under a row of large oak trees where he would remain in a sleep from which he could never wake.' The man doesn't realize how his son's death has changed him, but: 'His wife knew. His daughter knew. His friends knew.' It's his daughter who comes up with a way of commemorating the lost boy, which allows his father to begin rebuilding his life. The simplicity and grace of the story's final lines give me the chills every time I read them.

There are many joys to be found in this collection, but for me the greatest of them, and the most surprising, was that a generation often accused of being indifferent to the world, of being lost to their phones, should prove to be so passionately engaged with the world. They have their own truth to tell, and through the characters in these stories – weirdos, heros, jokers, ordinary folks like you and me, and, of course, Trippy – they are determined that you should hear them. They spent the best part of a year making their way here; now they are banging on your door.

Let them in.

Anger is a Killing Thing
Alicia Albu

"What has the world become when they let just anyone become a firefighter these days?" Papa said, as he scowled at a black man in a firefighter's uniform across the street from our diner.

"I'd run straight for the fire before he lay one of those dirty hands on me."

Feeling a hole where my stomach was, I tightened the grip on my glass at my father's latest comment. The rest of the table chuckled, only encouraging him.

" Just look at him! Blacker than the ace of spades!"

I cringed knowing that this was to be the topic of conversation for the rest of the night.

I stared at the ring on my left hand. This was the perfect moment to announce my engagement to Papa. He was in a good mood and, with all the eyes around, I hoped he would at least try to restrain himself a little from throwing profanities at me. The guilt had been eating at me for months now. He was going to find out eventually that the man I love is the kind he doesn't consider a man at all. I couldn't keep putting it off. My palms began to sweat and I swallowed hard. My heart hammered against my ribcage as I braced myself for what I was about to do.

"Papa," I managed to stutter.

"What is it Julia?" he said, bringing his attention on to me.

"I've gotten engaged."

Silence. Not a good start. My voice was barely audible as I delivered the punch.

"To a black man."

***

The whiteness of the room was blinding. My mind numb, along with the rest of my body. I felt slow, unable to process anything. It was like being in a trance, the constant beeping of a machine intensifying the effect.

My eyes wandered around the unfamiliar room before landing on an expectant Julia beside me, tears filling her red eyes.

Julia.

It was coming back to me now, flashes from the diner, the people, the conversations.

And then it hit me. I felt my insides heat up as reality dawned on me.

I started to shake with anger, how can she do this to me? How can my own daughter choose a bloody nigger over me? I should have seen this sooner, I've been raising a snake all these years! The beeping of the machine started to speed up.

"Papa, please! Calm down,"

she begged as she put her hand over my own. I yanked it away, disgusted.

"Get away! You're not my daughter!"

Hearing the commotion inside the room, a young looking doctor came in and was quick to try restore order.

"Sir, I'm afraid you can't be doing anything to raise your heart rate at the moment, I suggest you calm down before you make things worse."

"What? Why? What's going on?"

"Mr. Roberts, you've been out for a couple of days now. Your heart was unable to handle the stress it was put under and failed. You're a very lucky man though, it just so happened that we had a compatible donor available."

He paused, gauging my reaction.

I remained frozen, unable to wrap my head around what the doctor told me.

"The man's family has contacted me and requests to see who the heart of their loved one has saved. It would reassure them that they did the right thing," the doctor continued. My head started to pound. This was happening all too fast.

"In fact, they're here right now. They've been waiting all this time to meet you, Mr. Roberts. If you're ready I'd like for them to come in. They've spent enough time here at this hospital."

A pang of guilt came over me. These people had suffered enough. How could I ever repay them for giving me such a gift? I set all of my previous thoughts behind me and told the doctor to just bring them in now to get things over with.

I restrained myself from looking at Julia as the doctor went in search of the family. Seconds passed before he strolled back in the room. A black woman with three young children trailed behind him.

At that moment I felt the sky fall on top of me, crushing my lungs and knocking the air out of me.

Watching the scene unfold, I felt hot anger consume me. The heat, spreading through my body and taking over my mind. I could feel the hate radiating off me, filling the air around me, turning it red. The machine I was still attached to was now beeping urgently, trying to keep up with the rhythm of my heart. Seeing my reaction, the doctor ushered the savage with its offspring out of the room.

Julia was panicking, hovering over me with worry. By the time the doctor returned I was clawing at my ribcage in an idle attempt to get the alien object out of my body.

Walking towards me purposefully while fumbling around in his pockets to take out a syringe, he drove the needle into my arm and pried my hands away from my chest.

I felt the veins at my temples throb, but had no more time to react.

The sedative had already started to take its effect. I could no longer concentrate and lost my train of thought. The room began to blur around the edges. I fought hard to stay awake, to beg the doctor to take the disgusting thing out of me, but it was futile, the sedative was too strong and I gave in to the darkness.

***

At home Papa had seemed to improve. The doctor had told him something after waking up for the second time that seemed to have left an impression on him.

"Anger is a killing thing. It kills the man who let's it in, each rage leaving him less than he had been before - it takes something from him."

Hearing those words Papa grew stronger, unwilling to let the blacks rise victorious over him, to be defeated by them. No. Papa would never do that, he turned his curse into a blessing.

"I have their heart. I'm up here breathing and able to dance on their grave as they watch with jealousy in hell, where they belong."

I've been cautious the past few weeks not to anger him. Avoiding him - careful not to push the wrong button. Even though I love Papa, I must also think about my own happiness and marrying Max would bring me the greatest joy.

Max is the kind who sees the best in everyone, refusing to believe in evil. He thinks that he can change Papa, to make him see how wrong he was all these years. But there's no changing Papa. Max doesn't know the truth, how racist Papa can be, how much he hates him without ever needing to know him. I didn't want to worry him. Max is well raised though he feels the need to get a blessing from Papa to feel content with this marriage. I wish Papa would accept my wishes. To be walked down the aisle by my father, a dream every girl shares.

Taking a deep breath, I hold it in and knock on his bedroom door. I don't wait for an answer before entering, knowing he isn't asleep. He's in his bed, bible in hand. He didn't even look up to meet my eyes when I reach the foot of his bed, ignoring me. I have to make Papa see reason.

Max is waiting downstairs to finally meet his soon to be father-in-law.

He keeps reading on – oblivious to my presence. I feel like I'm invading his territory. Coils begin to tense in my stomach and I decide to try to ease into the topic.

I force myself to calm down, not wanting my voice to break or tremble, I want to be strong and brave.

"Papa. We should get a piano."

This seemed to get his attention as he lowers his book away from his face just enough to stare at me with a raised eyebrow.

I continue.

"You could learn a lot from it you know, piano keys are black and white, but they sound like a million colours in our head. The music can only be made when the keys are played together."

At the word 'black' I saw his knuckles turn white on the book. But I pressed on, determined to get my point across.

"Julia, if this is another one of your attempts to make me one of those nigger lovers, then you're wasting you're time. I know very well where you're going with this. Don't start."

"But Papa if you would just give him a chance! If you'd meet him you'd understand! You'll see, he's such a kind pers—"

"What?! You actually want me to meet that filth?"

"No, please just listen to me! All he wants is to meet you. You don't know how much it will mean to him if you would accept us. Please! I'll go bring him up so he can try talk to you as well. He's been waiting for such a long time!"

"You mean you brought that animal here. On my property. So it can tell me it wants to take you away from me?!"

His relatively calm demeanour starts to change as he processes the situation. His face contorts in anger, nostrils flaring, before he hides it under a cold mask. His eyes flash before narrowing into slits. I can see him straining to keep his control.

He silently reaches his arm under the bed, and pulls out a long, smooth piece of metal – his hunting rifle. I tremble. You can run your finger around the rim of a glass and it will make a sound. At this moment that's what I feel like. The sound of glass.

***

Leaping off the bed with my rifle, I race to the door. But before I can reach the handle Julia is there in front of me. She throws herself at my feet in a vain attempt to stop me. But it's too late. He triggered my fury, now I'll trigger a bullet through his head. Shaking her off, I continue to the stairs. I block Julia's way down the steps. She's close behind me. I can't let her pass. I need to get to my guest first for it to be a surprise.

Turning the corner to the living room I hear Julia's screaming pleas. They're underwater, drowned out by the storm inside my head. Pulling the door open I come face-to-face with the swine. I want to savour the look on his face when I blast a piece of metal through it.

I raise the rifle and cock it. His eyes widen and I can taste acid in my mouth. Before pulling the trigger, I feel a convulsion in my chest where my own heart used to be.

I steady my hand and shoot the gun, not wanting to waste any more time. Everything goes completely silent and all movement around me slows down to an excruciating pace as I watch Julia getting shot instead of him. To be the one to bleed instead of him.

I feel my pulse pounding through my body as I stare at the scene in front of me. He's hunched over Julia, covering her frame and touching her with his dirty hands, corrupting her body. Anger starts to fuel my flame once again. How dare he?! It's all his fault. Everything is always their fault, the dirt of the planet.

I point the gun towards him and pull the trigger once again. The metal fragments, spiralling through the air, pierced his chest and torso without consideration. The small wounds in his flesh leaked blood much like the way crying eyes leak tears. I don't feel remorse or sorrow as I watch him go out, falling on top of Julia.

I cringe inwardly and shove the limp corpse away from my daughter with the weapon that killed him. I gaze down on her face. Her eyes had been such a vivid blue in life that I was afraid to see what they looked like in death. They were closed now and she looked peaceful, like she was sleeping. Her pink lipstick was smeared around making it a grotesque mask against her now-pale skin.

There's nothing left for me to do now. No reason to continue. I point the gun to my chest, my mind hollow. The gunshot is not as loud as I had anticipated. I'm stunned to discover I'm dying and yet I am not overwhelmed by the emotion I assumed would accompany such a violent end. There's something altogether serene as I bleed out, a torrent flowing from my open wound. I smile. Images swirl before me right until the end, leaving that last scene of Julia's death imprinted upon my mind without the oxygen to sustain it. I stumble back and fall, now feeling a dulling pain in my chest. I am calm, unknowing of what is to come next, just that it is the end.

"Anger is a killing thing."

The Road

Laura Bourke

It all started with a bang. A bang that destroyed the world as we know it. I suppose I should rewind a bit and tell you what this bang actually was. Well about two weeks ago some messed up unemployed scientists were experimenting on bodies of people who had died from cancer thinking that they could find a cure for it.

Unfortunately they had completely miscalculated and ended up creating an army of undead. This my friends, is why you don't mess around with science and dead bodies Anyway they apparently heard this loud exploding noise and the bodies started to move. They hadn't created a cure to cancer; they'd created zombies.

The test subjects escaped and like any other stereotypical zombies they started infecting people with their bite. After a few hours there were thousands of people infected. This whole time I was sitting in my dump of a school, going between classes like any other day. It happened so quickly I don't think anyone even realized what was going on. People stormed in shouting that none of us were to leave the class, no matter what - that if we did 'they would get us'. Teachers were rounded up and informed on what was happening. Military officials turned up to the classes and we were put on lockdown. No one could get in and no one could leave.

We all thought they were trying to wind us up at first or that it was some hilarious prank on a game show - but then we looked out of our window and saw a dozen people walking around the edges of the school gate, their teeth glaring and hands clawing at the fences.

The only thing that was going through my mind at that minute was my family: my mum, dad and eleven-year-old brother who was being homeschooled. I knew I had to get out of there. It wasn't an option. My head was frantically making up plans and trying to block out the thought that they might already have been caught… Who knows what could have happened to them. I heard a groan beside me and turned to see my best friend Jake with his head in his hands. I knew that he was probably been thinking the same thing as me, worrying about the safety of his eight year old sister Rosie. Rosie meant the world to Jake. He cared so much about her and he was always trying to do everything he could to protect her. When Jake was eight his mum died while giving birth. He dedicated himself to bringing up Rosie and had never failed at that.

"Nicola… Where do you think our families are? What if they've been caught?" He asked me, nervously biting at his lip. I had never seen Jake worried before. Things were bad. He leaned over closer to me and whispered in my ear. "We're getting out of here right now. We have to go."

I nodded back while keeping an eye on our supervisor to make sure he couldn't see we were talking. Jake pointed his eyes towards the window beside my desk which looked out onto our schoolyard, and then to then to the field beyond it, which we walked to and from school every day.

"You're not serious are you? We'll be killed!" I murmured under my breath to him.

"Oh, I'm dead serious. It's a risk I'm willing to take. We have to get to them," he answered back.

I decided that it was no use arguing with him. He was right, we had to leave. I reached my arm out to open the window, earning myself a few stares from the people sitting around me.

"On the count of three…" he muttered to me. We slid our chairs out from underneath our desks and got into crouching positions, ready to pounce out of the window and run. Our supervisor glanced up to see what the movement was but never expected what happened next.

We jumped. Our supervisor screamed in horror and ran to the window trying to grab our flailing legs and pull us in but his efforts were in vain. We hit the ground with a thump.

"Are you okay?" Jake asked frantically, hopping up and brushing the dirt off of his trousers. I had cut my arm on a rock when I hit the ground and it was trickling blood. I grabbed the jumper of my sleeve and pulled it down.

"Yeah I'm good, it's just a scratch." I winced as Jake extended his arm to pull me up.

We stood up and looked towards our classroom. There was shouting and figures running around. The place was chaos. It seemed like we had started some sort of miniature revolution in the space of a minute. We decided to get out of there before anyone could catch up with us.

We didn't look back once. We ran through the dusty path surrounded by high grass that we had walked so many times before. Our feet tripped over rocks and were attacked by nettles but it was nothing compared to the creatures that were stumbling behind us. We turned the corner and saw a group of undead on the road ahead. We jumped back behind a car that was sitting in the middle of the road, while we decided how we would get past them. I took in my surroundings while trying to catch my breath and looked over to see Jake ripping parts off of the car.

"What are you doing? You're going to get us arrested!" I exclaimed trying to pull him away.

"I'm trying to save our lives," he whispered back pushing me away. "Now keep it down before they hear us." He kept pulling at the metal and finally he got two long strips off. "If they come near you, you'll have to hit them with this," he said, handing me what looked like the exhaust pipe of the car. He picked a registration plate up for himself and we leapt out from behind the car, making a run for the end of the road. I could hear the undead moaning; the sound of their feet dragging on the ground after us.

All of a sudden I felt something grab my back. It took hold of me and I couldn't shake it off. I turned round to see the rotting face of a middle aged woman. Her teeth glared. It was almost like time had frozen. She looked at me with a blank expression, like an animal about to kill its prey. I stood still unable to move while her watering mouth inched closer and closer to me.

It happened so quickly. An object slashed her head and she started bleeding while she dropped to the ground. I looked up to see Jake standing in front of me. His hand grabbed mine.

I could see our houses just up ahead and Jake signaled to head towards mine first. I started to get nervous as we approached it. What if they weren't there… or even worse what if they were there but had been bitten? My hand started to shake uncontrollably in Jake's.

He stopped me and put his hands on my shoulder. "Look even if they aren't in there it will be okay, we'll find them."

I hugged him and anxiously put my hand on the door knob.

The house was silent. "Is anyone here?" I called out but only to be greeted with my own echo. I fell to my knees with my head in my hands. Jake helped me over to the stairs where he sat me down.

"I'm going to have a look around, stay here."

I listened to his footsteps walking around the house. They stopped.

"Nicola.. Nicola! Come here."

I ran into the kitchen to see him holding a piece of paper. He handed it to me and I opened it to see my dad's messy scrawl. "Nicola, if you get to read this, help has come for us. We have left with Jake's family and a group of others. We are going to the city. They won't let us get you on the way as your school is on lockdown. We love you, never forget that"

I handed the note back to Jake who put it in his pocket. I ran up the stairs and shouted to him that I was packing clothes and blankets and that he would have to pack food. Jake didn't ask any questions as he knew what my plan was. We were going to the city.

"Nicola, I have to go to my house. There is something I can't leave without. Ill hop over the back fences so I won't have to go out on the road," he called up to me.

"Just be careful please," I pleaded.

Just after I heard the door close I started to realize how much of an idiot I was. Why had I let him go by himself? Who knew what sort of danger was in his house. What if one of the undead had gotten in and attacked him? I was panicking that he wouldn't come back at all. I couldn't do this by myself. My legs started to go limp with worry, collapsing underneath me.

A moment later I heard the door open and to my relief he was back. He was carrying a teddy bear in his hand which I recognized instantly. It was Rosie's teddy that Jake had gotten her when she was born. I had always wondered how she could be attached to a bear that was missing an arm, but I suppose that's just what kids do.

"She left it in the house… I have to bring it to her," he said quietly.

I nodded, understanding.

***

We left the house with our bags of supplies planning to get a car. We didn't want to take one of our parent's ones as it didn't feel right to steal a car from our family. We found a car up the road from us that was filled with petrol. Luckily the owner for some bizarre reason kept a key in the passenger door. It was a large car so it would offer as transport and shelter for us.

"Guess them driving lessons dad gave me are finally paying off," Jake laughed, Opening the door.

Just as we were getting into the car we heard a knocking noise. We looked round to see our twelve-year-old neighbor Charlie looking out at us. She opened the window and called out that she was going to climb down, and if we could catch her if she fell. When she got down she explained all that had happened to us. Everyone else had either fled or was no longer living…

"Thank you so much for not just leaving…" She said. "I had to watch the troops gather up everyone and leave without me because I didn't get back to the house on time. I heard my mum screaming that they had to wait for me to come back. But they didn't. I went straight back to my house and locked myself in my bedroom. I was too afraid to go out and find other people. "

We told Charlie that we were going to where everyone had been taken and that she could come with us. We started driving following signs for the city, flicking through radio stations to see if we could find anything being broadcasted but there was nothing. Jake knew from going to the city before that it would be about four hours, so we set up camp for the night. Dark approached fast and the only light we had was from the few surrounding street lamps that had turned on. I covered the seats of the car with blankets for Charlie and Jake to sleep on while I took guard watching for the first few hours

I searched around in cars near us and got more supplies that we could use, even after a few hours of traveling our canned foods were starting to run out and I knew we couldn't survive on pineapple in a tin forever. I was killing off the undead that approached our camp by slashing them through the head, feeling even guiltier each time, as these people had families at one stage who loved and cared about them. They would never want to see them like this.

I heard the door of the car open and looked over to see Charlie getting out. "I'm just going to the toilet I'll be back in a minute," she murmured under her breath, so we wouldn't attract any attention from the dead. Her eyes were heavy in her head probably from all that had happened in the last twenty four hours. She rubbed them while yawning, trying to keep herself alert and awake. I watched her from the corner of my eye walking into the bushes closest to our little camp.

For a minute, there was only the sound of the wind swirling around the trees. Then all of a sudden, high pitched screams of terror pierced the air. Jake poked his head out of the car, wrapped in a blanket that used to sit on his couch in his sitting room, trying to keep warm despite the freezing temperatures. "Please tell me that wasn't her," he said, panic showing on his face.

We ran towards the bushes using a torch that I had found nearby to see in front of us, following the screams of pain to where we found her. There was an undead body thrashing on the ground tangled in roots and branches from the surrounding trees. Charlie was on the ground beside it struggling to get away but it had its arms wrapped tight around her and was chewing on her leg. She was covered in blood and the tears were streaming down her face. Jake tore apart the monsters head and I grabbed her out of the reach of him.

"I'm going to die; I'll never get to see my family again," She cried.

Carrying her towards the car we tried to reassure her that she would be fine – but we knew we were lying to her and to ourselves.

When we reached the car we lay her out on a blanket on the ground. Her leg was bloody and she was getting weaker with every minute that passed. Jake was wrapping her leg in bandages, and doing the best he could, tried to stop the bleeding while I wiped tears from her face.

Before we knew it she was gone. Jake grabbed a shovel from the boot while I gathered flowers from the roadside and wrapped her up. We couldn't bring ourselves to wait until she came back as one of them so we buried her while she was still temporarily gone.

Neither of us slept that night but we got up early the next morning and continued on our journey. Street signs told us that we were about forty kilometres away. We stopped at midday and had something to eat but continued on as we knew we were near. It was eerily quiet the whole time; Jake and I didn't say much to each other.

Both of us were slumped tiredly in the front seats of the car when we saw it ahead of us. Makeshift walls of cars and fencing boarded together surrounded the area. They were arranged around a group of buildings. Jake suddenly jolted the car to a stop, both of us springing up to have a look at what we would be entering.

"Should we circle around first just to make sure there's no actual danger?" he asked me, a mixture of excitement and nervousness on his face.

We reversed the car back down the road a bit a drove around it, looking from afar. When we agreed that it looked safe we approached the gates. They were made of heavy iron gates that looked to be at least three metres high. We got out of the car and walked up to the gates, not wanting to look like we were a threat. This is exactly the type of place our families would be safe in.

We saw people inside the gates start looking out at us and pointing. We felt like animals in a zoo being watched, except we were the ones outside of the fences. The gates started to inch open, just enough for a person to fit through. A group of men carrying an assortment of weapons came out and ran behind us, killing the undead that had been attracted by the sound.

"Are you sure about this?" Jake asked nervously.

"Yes. This is it," I replied, feeling the excitement kicking in.

We got out of the car to meet a man who introduced himself as Pete. He explained that he was in charge of the day to day running of the place. He told us how as soon as the outbreak started to happen they got everyone they could and started building makeshift walls around a group of buildings. They had been calling it home since. It had been hard with so many people living in such a small place. Food had been hard to get but they raided local supermarkets every day.

He got us a hot meal, something we hadn't had in a while, and while we were eating asked how we knew to go to the city center. We told him that our families had left a note to us that we discovered after breaking out of our school. When we told him who our families were his face lit up. "No way… it's you! Your families are here, come with me now and I'll bring you too them."

And so he did. He brought us to them and it was the happiest moment of our lives. We all broke down in tears, embracing them like there was no tomorrow. It was a miracle that we were all safe and reunited.

They had a perfect place to stay, and their every need was cared for. And here I am eight years later, telling you my story. The place has grown by thousands of people and the walls have been expanded massively. We are doing our best to find a cure, using every facility we have available. Although the threat of being bitten is just outside of the walls, the undead are slowly dying off. The world is returning to what it used to be.

Trippy's Travels

Luke Collins

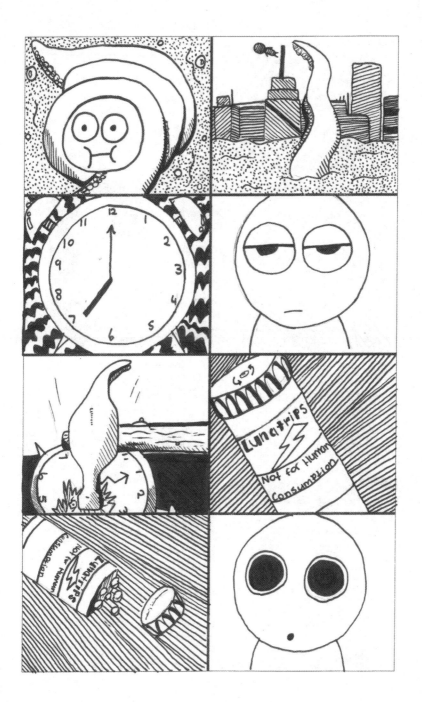

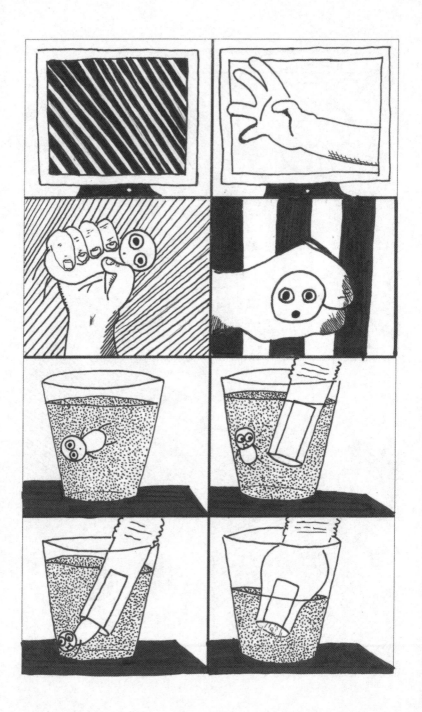

The Unexpected Hero
Matthew Dolan

Anna was sprinting through dark alleys. She could feel the presence of the beast rather than hear it as it was almost silent when it ran. As she turned a corner and ran past more dust bins, she slipped on something and fell hard to the ground. She turned just in time to see the beast round the corner. She looked frantically around for something to defend herself with and saw the beer bottle that she had fallen on. Just as she reached for it she was pinned by the beast's powerful hands. It was upon her, fangs bared. She knew this was it but was determined to not go down without a fight.

***

Earlier that day Anna woke to the sound of her mother's voice calling up the stairs, "Anna, hurry up or else we'll be late and you know how your father hates that."

She hauled herself out of bed and pulled on the dress her mother had left out for her. She absolutely hated wearing dresses but this was her Aunt Louise's wedding. Her very rich aunt. And everyone attending wanted to be at their very best to make sure she was happy because there was a very nice beach house at stake that everyone was sure was in the will. Anna hated being around her Aunt Louise because she was so stuck up and treated Anna like a child. Adults could be so greedy sometimes, they were all perfectly well-off people but as usual they wanted to have another house or a more expensive car or something like that. People only like her cause she's rich. Anna thought to herself.

***

An hour later the three of them were driving down the motorway when Anna's mam realised she had forgotten her purse. Cursing loudly Anna's dad pulled off the motorway and headed for the nearest bank. The whole way there Anna had to listen to the two of them bickering about whose fault it was that she had forgotten it. The argument culminated with Anna's mam slamming the car door as she got out in the bank car park. Anna got out too saying that she needed to go to the bathroom. She walked into the bank with her mother and while she was waiting in the queue Anna walked down a corridor and into the bathroom.

Just as she was about to turn on the tap to wash her hands she heard the unmistakable sound of gunfire from outside. Anna hurried to the door and opened it just enough to see a small area of the bank. There was her mother huddled beside a pale man with a large hat that obscured most of his face. Then a tall man in a ski mask walked in front of them. He was carrying a sawed-off shotgun in one hand and held a grenade in the other. As he moved down the hall towards her the man in the large hat looked up and signaled to her to move back into the bathroom. A moment later she could hear the robbers footsteps on the other side of the door. He was going to check the bathroom for other civilians he could use as hostages to get a nice fat payoff. As she heard the door creak open and then a crash as the pale man sprinted up behind the robber and slammed him into the door and then a bang that echoed around the bathroom as the robber attempted to shoot the unexpected hero. The second the robber looked at Anna he hissed and beard his teeth as he struggled against the lock the pale man had him in. then as she watched him struggle his teeth lengthened and became long pointed fangs. With immense speed and strength he pushed away from the man and jumped at Anna. In that second her mind went blank and instinctively she stuck out her hands to try and protect herself when she did this, however, there was a rippling sensation that emitted from Anna's palms, then a whooshing sound like a strong wind then the man was lifted from the ground and smashed through the walls of two stalls before landing unconscious in a toilet. Anna had closed her eyes when the man had jumped but opened them slowly to see the carnage that had previously been a bathroom. She saw the robber unconscious in a stall directly opposite her and looked around at the pale man who had pinned the robber against the door. His mouth was open in astonishment and he looked like someone had smacked him in the face.

"How long have you been able to do that?" the pale man asked in astonishment.

"Do what?" Anna replied perplexed.

"Magic," he said in barely more than a whisper.

Anna didn't know what to think. She tried to deny it but how else could a sixteen year old girl have thrown a grown man through two walls.

"Just there," she said slowly. "That's the first time I've ever done anything like that."

"Let's get out of here, there will be more arriving soon," the man said as he hauled the robber out of the toilet.

She followed behind him all the way up the hall back into the bank to cheers and applause of the would-have-been hostages. He directed everyone out of the bank and followed by Anna walked back in sat the unconscious robber in the bank managers chair, pulled the pin on the grenade and place it carefully behind the robbers back so that if he was moved it would blow up then he and Anna strode out of the bank.

Before Anna could say more than thank you the man strolled off into the ally beside the bank and was gone. Anna walked over to the corner and looked down the dark, smelly alley expecting to see him only a few feet ahead of her but to her surprise he was gone.

***

A while later Anna and her family were sitting around a small table in a petrol station drinking a cup of tea to calm down after what had been an 'extremely stressful experience' as Anna's mam put it. She thought she had had the worst of it but Anna hadn't told her parents about her newfound ability. They were considering whether or not to go to the wedding dinner as they had already missed the ceremony. Anna insisted she was fine and wanted to go when they asked. This would give her the perfect chance to sneak off and practice he skill. Grudgingly her parents agreed and they were off again to the hotel.

***

Later that night, at the hotel the wedding party was being held in, Anna headed up to the room she and her parents were staying in as they were completely drunk and incapable of speech, let alone driving. So she went upstairs and got changed out of her dress and into a t-shirt and a pair of jeans in which she felt far more comfortable. She decided to go for a walk to the shops in the village up the road as it was quite a warm night. As Anna walked down the pathway that led from the gates to the front doors of the hotel, she felt like she was being watched so turned and looked back up the path towards the hotel but saw nothing but the lit windows of the restaurant and bedrooms and the apple trees that lined the path. She made it to the main gate without anymore weird feelings, but then from behind the tall pillar beside her, a tall, extremely pale man strode out. Although Anna was startled by his sudden appearance, she thought that this man looked quite like the man who had saved her in the bank. He too was abnormally pale but this man looked as though there wasn't a drop of blood in his entire body. He was bald but had scars all over his head and face and was wearing a crisp black suit and altogether did not look like he should be hiding behind pillars at twelve o'clock at night.

"Hello, Anna," he said in a deep but smooth voice that did not make Anna feel any safer. "You've had quite an eventful day today, haven't you?"

"How do you know my name?" blurted Anna.

"Oh, Anna," he replied, "you have been quite the topic of conversation today in my... family.

"You see," he continued taking no notice of Anna backing away slowly, "that man you killed earlier, he was my brother and the two men who went to collect him after his distress call was sent out they were my brothers too. All blown to pieces," he explained "and you see I don't take kindly to people killing my family members."

"I didn't kill anyone," Anna explained hastily, "it was that tall guy in the hat set the grenade." She explained still not taking her eyes off the man but she had stopped backing away.

"Well that grenade that he set went off as my brother was moved. Even if you didn't kill him you are an accessory to murder which is still punishable." said the man with a manic gleam in his eye.

"What?" he hissed, he had been distracted for a moment and didn't see the connection, "a tall man in a hat set the trap?"

"Yeah, yeah he saved me from your brother."

"Well then that changes things," he said with another gleam in his eye. "Well it doesn't change your predicament. I'm still going to kill you." he put emphasis on the last word. "But it changes mine. Oh well, better get to it then."

"Wow, wait… what?" Anna stammered.

"Oh yes, you killed my brothers so I shall kill you. You know an eye for an eye and all that." He said with a small laugh.

"Anyway let's get to it cause I'll have to deal with that meddlesome vampire slayer as well tonight."

This was all way too much for Anna to process but she knew one thing for certain, this man wanted to kill her. She turned on her heels and ran for her life.

***

She was sprinting down a deserted street. She knew she needed to get to the busier part of town and find someone who could help her, but she knew in the back of her mind she wouldn't make it but pushed that thought aside and ran. But still she didn't turn to see the distance between her and what was now a fully fledged vampire. The thing chasing after her bore no resemblance to any man. It had huge pointed teeth. Two of which were almost double the length of the others and the scars on his head stood out all over its head. Its legs grew and feet elongated and burst through the shoes he had been wearing. It could run faster and cover larger distances and ran almost silently. She made it into the village but had to get towards the shops before she would have any chance of survival because there she could use the alleys to get the vampire lost in.

Anna was sprinting through dark alleys. She could feel rather than hear the vampire closing in on her. As she turned a corner and ran past more dust bins, she slipped on something and fell hard to the ground. She turned just in time to see the vampire round the corner. She looked around for something to defend herself with and saw the beer bottle she had slipped on. Just as she reached for it she was pinned by the vampire's powerful claws as it was upon her, fangs bared. She knew this was it but was determined not to go down without a fight. She tried everything possible to summon her powers but nothing happened. Then suddenly there was a familiar rushing sound, like wind. She knew she had used magic but then her stomach dropped as she realized with a shock of horror that the vampire hadn't moved. It was too heavy and her weak wind was not going to move it. She knew the moon above her would be the last thing she would ever see before she was saved. But then a shadowy figure obscured the moon in between the two buildings and somehow she knew it was here to help her, whatever it was. It landed with a dull thud directly behind the vampire but it didn't hear it as it was too preoccupied with Anna. Not until the figure behind it drew a silver revolver from beneath its cloak and cocked it did the vampires refined sense of hearing notice it was there, well, that and the figure had the gun pressed against the creatures head. The figure spoke in a voice Anna vaguely recognised.

"Release the girl and stand up slowly." Anna questioned the figures motives at first, trying to reason with a monster, but to her overwhelming relief and surprise, the vampire released her and stood up to face the hooded figure. Then without warning and with extremely fast reflexes, knocked the gun from the figures hand and speared him to the ground; unconscious. With the force he hit the ground his hood had slipped off and Anna could see the pale face of the man who had saved her life and the life of all the people in the bank earlier that day.

Without even thinking Anna snatched the gun from the ground beside a large, dirty dumpster and turned ready to fire. But there was nothing there. She looked up and down the ally but there was no sign of the vampire. Then from above her she heard a scraping noise and some panting. Anna looked up to see the vampire scaling the building with immense speed. She raised the gun. Steadied her hands, which had been shaking violently. Got the creatures head between the sights and fired. There was two seconds in which time seemed to freeze and the vampire was still. Then gravity took over and it fell, fast. Then with a sickening crunch and a thump that shook the ground, the beast landed, still and dead. Anna felt the rush of adrenaline surge through her veins after the shot. Just then the pale mans eyelids flickered and he stirred. Anna heard him moving and darted to his side as his eyes opened drowsily.

"You again?" he muttered.

"Yep, me again," Anna replied, "I do seem to have a knack for getting into trouble." She said smartly. She offered him a hand and he grasped it as she pulled him off the ground.

"Anna," she said as she stuck out her hand and he shook it. "Blaze."

"Blaze?" Anna enquired, "That's an unusual name."

"Not as unusual as the world you have just been forced into. Believe me," he responded with a smirk as they strode back up the dirty, dingy, smelly ally, back to the mortal world where vampires were safely trapped inside storybooks and had no idea how close their world had come to merging with the world of monster and magic.

"Does that happen often?" Anna asked, "You know, a man turning into one of them… things."

"More often than I care to mention, Anna." Blaze responded with a grim smile.

"I'm going to need you to come with me," said Blaze as he dusted himself off.

"Where? Wait, I can't I have to get back to the hotel, my parents will know I'm missing."

"Your parents?" Blaze said with a smile "I've been watching you closely after the incident at the bank and from what I can see your parents are as they say nowadays, 'smashed out of their heads.'"

Anna laughed but remained weary, "Where are we going?"

"It's not far from here. About a five minute walk."

"Oh, I forgot to mention. Now you know you have powers you have to be registered."

"Registered?" said Anna in surprise "It must be a big world of magic if you have to keep tabs on people."

"Oh it is. About a quarter of a million people last time I checked. And that's just in Ireland, there are sorcerers in almost every country in the world."

"Wow!" Anna said in disbelief as they started to walk.

They had been walking for almost exactly five minutes, just chatting. Anna found out that Blaze used to be a vampire himself but turned on them after they used him as a lab rat for an experiment to remove the vampire from him and make him mortal but it had been excruciatingly painful and he was still left extremely pale. But for the most part it had worked and now he worked directly for the greatest sorcerer and ruler of their time; Balrog. He worked for him killing or imprisoning vampires. He explained that is why they robbed the bank, to get money to fund their experiments to make vampires stronger and create an army to overthrow Balrog and take control of the magical race.

They came across a small, seemingly abandoned cottage down a quiet laneway. Blaze walked right up to it and opened the front door and stood back to let Anna through. "My mam always warned me against going into deserted cottages with strange vampire slayers," Anna said as she walked passed him into the cottage.

"God, your mother is awfully specific," said Blaze with a smile. Blaze walked into the sitting room and without hesitation stepped into the fireplace, completely unaware of how peculiar it looked. There was no fire lit as the cottage was empty but still looked strange. He told Anna to step in too. She did so and before she had time to make herself comfortable in the cramped space it began to descend.

Then before she knew it she was in a huge room bathed in an orange glow from the chandelier of candles hanging from the roof. Compared to the musty cold feeling of the cottage above this room could not have been more of a contrast. It was warm and had a cozy feeling to it. The walls were lined with shelves of books. And at the end of the room, there was a huge mahogany desk with paper piled high that almost obscured the man sitting behind it.

He was a plump man with a long grey beard and moustache; he wore magnificent black robes streaked with silver. As he peered around the stack of paper he beamed and let out a shout, "Blaze!"

"Balrog!" Blaze replied just a cheerily.

"I see you've brought a friend."

"Yes Balrog, a newly-discovered."

"Oh it's been a while since we've had one of those in this office," Balrog said with a surveying look at Anna. "That's not usually my department, why bring her to me?"

"I believe she may have certain…qualities," Blaze explained.

"Well then come right over here, young lady," Balrog said as he ushered her towards him.

Anna moved slowly, glancing back at Blaze. When Anna was standing in front of Balrog, he looked her up and down for about thirty seconds, then suddenly he raised his hands and before Anna could object or move back he placed them over her ears, arms outstretched and eyes closed in concentration. A moment later he released her as if she had given him an electric shock.

"Are you okay?" Anna asked hurriedly, worried that she had hurt him.

"Yes, yes my dear just fine…but…" he trailed off.

"What is it Balrog? Is it what I expected?" Blaze asked hurriedly with increasing excitement.

"Blaze," he said in a whisper, "I don't think any of us expected this. My dear I believe you are a Descendant."

"What? Descended from who?" Anna asked confused.

"The great race of sorcerers that lived many thousands of years ago."

"That explains it!" exclaimed Blaze. "She killed the vampire king!"

"In full transformation? Balrog said in astonishment.

"In full transformation," replied Blaze.

"But that was just the silver bullet; you said that's the only thing that can kill a vampire, Blaze," Anna said confused.

"It is, but the bullet in the gun wasn't silver. It was led, just a normal bullet. Only an extremely powerful sorcerer could have changed something like that," Blaze explained.

Anna was in shock. She hardly heard anything that was said after that. Before she knew it, it was a week later and she was a national heroine in the magical world but was still a quiet nobody in the 'other world', as Anna had taken to referring to it as.

And for many years after that night she was still removing the monsters that were vampires, from the world with Blaze at her side.

No Man's Land
Dylan Forde

Dear Diary   *June 16th 2012*   *11:46am*

I'm sitting here in this empty blank flat staring out the window taking in every last detail I had never noticed before. The feeling of emptiness inside killing me off. I never thought I'd see the day when I would be saying goodbye to my life as I've known it for all this time but it's for the best.

Bags packed, Passport ready to be stamped. Taxi will arrive any minute now. It's goodbye to Dublin and my sorry existence here, but hey! What other option do I have? Four years of university and now two years later, still not a sniff of a job.

Anyway it's about time I cut the apron strings. My parents have been a great help, maybe a little too much. Shit, there's the taxi! (Talk later?)

Dear Diary   *June 18th 2012*   *8:31am*

It is two days since the crash. All I can remember is coughing up sand and sea water, as I gasped for air. I cried for help as I struggled to my feet. I scanned the beach but it was deserted. I fell numerous times as I ran up the beach. The beach was endless. I stopped and turned to be met by a vast blue ocean for miles and miles. Walking out into the ocean, I splashed my face with water to wake up from this nightmare but the frightening thing was that this was my reality. Then I spotted my carry-on bag, with you, this diary in it. Now I know I'm not alone.

Dear Diary   *June 19th 2012*   *7:15am*

I slept on the beach last night. It was a calm and quiet night, not a sound to be heard but for the rustling of the trees in the cool breeze. I found a nice quiet spot beneath the stars. Whilst staring at the stars my mind started rambling and making me think about my family and how I am going to get off this island! Has anybody realised I'm gone? Surely I can't be the only survivor? What if there isn't even a search? Surely I'm going to be found within the next day or so! I hope my family are okay. I was passing out with the tiredness but my thoughts kept me awake staring at the dawn of a new day, hopefully it will bring me luck and a way of the island. As the sun continued to burn down on my sweltering body I luckily had a 250ml bottle of water in my carry-on. Food on the other hand will be a different matter; I had better start looking fast.

Dear Diary   *June 19th 2012   5:22pm*

Just back from looking and I'm really starting to panic but I'm trying my best to keep calm. I found nothing of worth, like food or water and by the heat of this sun I'm going to have nothing left in my bottle. Talking to you is keeping me from worrying right now because I'm trying to stay as positive as I possibly can. It's just you and I all alone on this never-ending beach surrounded by Rocky Mountains and facing this vast blue sea. I've got to find a new location for now to hold up on for at least a day or two. I can be attacked by wild animals on the island at any time if I don't get to a vantage point. I need to establish somewhere safe.

Dear Diary   *19th June 2012   10:22pm*

It's later in the day since we last talked and I have found a small dark cave at the top of the beach. The smell of seaweed in the cave is disgusting but at least it seems safe and I have somewhere to sleep tonight. It's starting to get dark and I have no source of light in this cave what so ever, so fire is going to be another problem…

Dear Diary   *20th June 2012   1:05pm*

I haven't written since yesterday and I've got to find a water source or else I will not survive, it's as simple as that. I'm gonna go looking for water because I have nothing left in my bottle, I think I'll head further in to the forest area because there has got to be a water source somewhere in there. I haven't had any sort of water in the last day or two and I'm starting to feel very tired and weak. I better start looking fast…

Dear Diary   *20th June 2012*   *6:32pm*

Just back from searching and I found a small stream coming down through the rocks. It's no Ballygowan but that water felt like the best thing I've ever tasted, I could just feel it slowing going down my throat…I could have drank this place dry with the thirst! Tonight I'm going to rest up well and find whatever source of food I possibly can. I can only imagine what I would be like to just be sitting in a nice warm restaurant waiting to be served a delicious hot meal. Cutting in and taking the first bite, the taste bursting from the meat as it slowly goes down my throat and into my hungry stomach. If only it was that easy…

Dear Diary   *21st June 2012*   *9:52am*

I'm going to set out again to find a source of food somewhere, anywhere, anything will do, I just need to eat. I feel dead inside and the most important thing at this stage is to keep mentally strong. Please God bring me some luck.

Dear Diary   *22nd June 2012*   *1:13pm*

It's six days since the crash and still no sign of a boat, plane or a helicopter. Like have they already found the other survivors and they forgot about me? What if everyone else is dead and they think I am too? What if I'm left here forever? I am left to die on this island. My family don't know where I am, I bet they are distraught not knowing where I am and thinking I'm dead. If only I could just see them one more time to tell them I'm alive.

Dear Diary   *22nd June 2012*   *8:03pm*

I searched most of the beach today and I found two small turtles crawling along the shore. I ran over with a sharp branch and pressed down hard on their shells in order to crack them. I ate them raw and it wasn't pleasant but at least I've got something in my stomach to last another day or two. I've got to make fire...

Dear Diary   *23rd June 2012*   *6:19pm*

Today I tried to make fire by using dry leaves on the ground in a little pit I dug. I tried for hours but nothing seemed to work. Not even a spark. I'm not going to give up.

Dear Diary   *24th June 2012*   *7:21pm*

I kept at it again but still no fire…

Dear Diary   *26th June 2012*   *2:00pm*

I keep trying to make fire but I can't even get it light yet, this seems impossible.

Dear Diary   *27th June 2012*   *9:33am*

Last night I was thinking about the three things I would love most that I could have right now, 1. Toilet roll, 2. Fire Lighters, 3. Mr. Cuddles, My one and only teddy bear I've had all my life, never have I needed him more.

Dear Diary   *27th June 2012*   *9:42pm*

Still no fire…

Dear Diary   *22nd June 2012*   *9:56pm*

Today I kept trying to make fire. Haven't much food either but my main focus right now is to make fire, it's vital I because if I continue eat meat I need to cook it or else I could die of food poisoning. Making fire is also vitally important to draw attention to any boats or planes passing by in the distance.

Dear Diary   *25th June 2012   11:04pm*

Today was spent trying to make fire again, still no luck…

Dear Diary   *26th June 2012   9:12pm*

Hey! I'm just finished after another day of trying to make fire and guess what? I made fire! Today is finally the day that I made fire and it is a marvellous day. No more lying in the dark wet cave for me.

Dear Diary   *27th June 2012   10:11am*

Last night I got a really goodnight's sleep for once due to the small fire that was made and it kept the cave from being so cold as it usually is. Today I'm going to make SOS signals on the beach using branches that have fallen off the trees. I haven't noticed many planes or boats that go by but there's got to be some out there, like I can't be all alone here I just can't be! Better head off and make some signs, talk later

Dear Diary   *31st June 2012   3:13am*

Haven't talked in a few days because all I've been doing is making SOS signs on the beach trying to get ships or planes that are going by to notice me but so far nothing seems to be happening. I also haven't been sleeping much either because I keep getting dreams of being back home and sitting at the dinner table with my whole family eating pizza like we always did on a Saturday night. Every time I go to hug my mam, and it's always my mam, I always wake up sweating like I just had a bad nightmare but I'm waking up into a nightmare. I've been on this island twenty-nine days today and it's only been in the past few days that I've been getting these dreams of being back home. I got to get off this island…

Dear Diary   *6th August 2012   4:12pm*

I haven't written in a week according to the days in my diary but for the past week I've been building a small boat made out of broken branches and weaves tied around them to keep it all together. I haven't tried it out yet but I hope it floats!

Dear Diary   *12th August 2012   12:01pm*

Today is my final day here, whether I make it alive or not I've got to get off this island I'm leaving you behind here and hopefully one day you will be found...

Apartment Block 3
Rebecca Kelly

Floor 7

Room 27B

16:29

Jamie was slouched lazily on the couch, mindlessly browsing the internet with the T.V buzzing quietly in the background. He was so bored. His boyfriend, Matthew, was supposed to be home from college over an hour ago. He wasn`t even answering any of his text messages. Jamie was worried. He knew he was probably far too over-protective, but he had reason to be. Matthew had been getting a pretty hard time at college lately. The "popular group" had caught them out on a date a couple of months back and had been giving him shit about it ever since. It was mainly just stupid name-calling, but Jamie had spotted a couple of cuts and bruises. Matthew just brushed it off but it was obviously starting to get to him. He used to love going to class every day, but now Jamie had to practically drag him out of bed every morning. It was extremely upsetting to watch someone so kind and happy and just a genuinely nice person be bullied for something he couldn`t ever change. And even if he could, why should he? It made Jamie's` blood boil. How in this day and age could people be so horrible, so ignorant that—

Jamie was snapped out of his train of thought and back into reality when he heard the door click open. Quickly throwing his laptop to one side and jumping up excitedly, he ran towards the door.

"Matthew! Where have you been, I was…" Jamie began calling out before he reached his boyfriend who was slumped against the closed door. His stomach churned, it was even worse than he had thought. There in front of him stood his worst nightmare. The man he loved, battered and broken.

"Jesus Christ, Matt!" he whispered in shock before rushing over to help. He gazed across Matthew's ripped clothes and bruised skin as he bit back tears. This was worst yet.

"Oh Matt," Jamie sighed as he pulled him into a gentle hug, trying not to hurt the poor boy any more than he already was. Jamie's heart wrenched when he felt Matthew's warm tears on his shoulder.

"Shh, it's okay, you're okay," he shushed Matthew before gently tilting his chin up so he could see his face. Jamie gasped. It was horrible. Matthews' deep chocolate eyes, that were usually so bright and happy, were now bloodshot and glazed over with tears. There was a deep purple bruise begging to form over his left eye and his lip was split and bleeding. The thing that upset Jamie the most though was the three big letters written in black marker pen right across Matthew's forehead. "FAG".

He snapped. He couldn't control himself. He was furious.

"What have they done to you? I'm going to kill those bastards!" Jamie screamed. Rage surged through his entire body and he clenched his fists in anger. He would have marched right out of the door and gone searching for those low lives, if his boyfriend wasn't clinging to the handle for support. Jamie realized his little outburst wasn't helping an already bad situation. He took a few deep breaths to calm himself down before turning his attention back to Matthew.

"Come on, let's get you cleaned up," Jamie said, already making his way back down the hallway. He turned back around when he reached the sitting room to find Matthew still slouched against the door.

"I-I don't t-think I can walk too w-well, I'm s-sorry," Matthew stuttered out.

Jamie cursed himself. How could he be such an idiot? He quickly made his way over and wrapped an arm around Matt's waist, slowly but surely guiding him to the bathroom. Matthew sat himself down onto the closed lid of the toilet seat. He let out a shaky breath as he tried to get comfortable on the cold, hard, plastic seat. Every inch of his body ached and stung from where he was used as a human punch bag. In that moment he wanted nothing more than for the ground to open up and swallow him. He felt like complete and utter shit. He managed to force a small smile when Jamie returned with his hands full of first aid supplies, looking flustered.

"Okay I'm going to need you to tell me what happened so I can help," Jamie told Matthew while softly rubbing his shoulder. Matthew didn`t want to talk about it. He shook his head quickly hoping to get his point across before he was stopped by his pounding headache that he just made a lot worse.

Eventually, after a few more kisses and kind words, Jamie had manage to persuade Matt into telling him what had happened. They were both sat on the cold, tiled floor as it was slightly more comfortable than the cheap, plastic toilet set when Matthew began to speak.

"Well, I-I was walking t-to the bus stop and I heard s-someone call my name a-and when I t-turned around t-they were all s-standing there," Matthew explained in a shaky voice.

"How many of them were there?" Jamie asked, although he was too almost afraid to find out.

"Nine," Matthew replied blankly before shifting slightly so he was leaning more of his body weight against the wall than before.

Jamie gulped. Nine. NINE PEOPLE? The thought made him sick to his stomach.

"They started off shouting things at me, as usual" Matthew said continuing with his story, "it was fine though, I could ignore them. But one of them, he just wouldn`t give up. He kept shouting in my face and blocking my way, and I just snapped and…" Matthew drifted off towards the end.

Jamie raised an eyebrow. Sweet and all as Matt was, when it came to conflict he had an array of snarky remarks and bitchy comments that he would spew out at anyone who was bothering him.

"What did you say?" Jamie questioned.

"I told him 'I'm no expert in cacti, but you sir, are a prick!' Or something stupid like that, I'm sorry `kay," Matthew mumbled.

"And you thought that would help the situation?" Jamie asked with a giggle.

"You`re an idiot, you know that right?" he told Matthew with a smile as he leant down to place a kiss on the other boys forehead. Matthew laughed leaning into the kiss and closing his eyes.

"Yeah, well I'm your idiot so you`re stuck with me forever," he said opening his eyes again. Seeing the smile on his face and the joy in his voice Jamie decided not to ruin Matthew's happiness by asking any more questions just yet. He gave Matt another quick peck on the lips before grabbing the first aid kit and returning to his side.

"Let`s see if I can find a sexy beast underneath all of that blood and dirt!" Jamie spoke over-dramatically as he brought a washcloth up to Matthew's face.

"Oh my GOD you`re so embarrassing," Matthew complained as his boyfriend continued washing his face and laughing at his own stupid jokes...

Room 26B

16:52

Doris smiled when she heard the two younger boys next door laughing and giggling to themselves. Although, she couldn`t help but feel a pang of jealousy. She didn`t have the same thing as they did, and at this stage in life, probably never would.

Doris was in her late seventies and had been married to her husband, John, since they were both in their early twenties.

She would be lying if she said she had never been in love with him, she was, but that love died a long time ago. Doris had fallen head-over-heals for John, what she didn`t realise at the time was that she had landed in a sixty-foot-deep hole which was impossible to climb out of.

John had always liked a drink. Who didn't? Doris never considered it a problem. But as time dragged on his bad habits just grew worse. He had transformed into a rage-filled alcoholic by the time he was in his late thirties. He was no longer the man Doris loved, just a monster living in the same skin.

They never had children, which was something Doris had always regretted. All her family had either left or passed away. Doris didn't even have a friend. Not one single friend! This was mainly due to the fact that John wouldn't let her leave the flat without him. And every other minute of the day she was working. She did all the cooking, cleaning, ironing, everything that needed to be done, she did. John never lifted a finger, and if he ever did it was only to grab another can of beer or to change the channel onto something even more dull and boring than he was watching before.

Doris always smiled and put on a happy face even though she was wasting every moment of her life waiting on a monster who drained any sort of hope she had left. Still, they both carried on the act of being the "picture perfect" couple. The trouble with a picture is that it only shows one tiny moment in time, and that moment had past long ago.

People always thought they were the cutest couple around, walking everywhere in linked arms, John always knowing what Doris wanted in the local pub. What everyone failed to realise was that it was all a lie. Nobody noticed how tight Johns' grip was, nobody saw the bruises, nobody heard the hateful words, no-body but Doris. And although nobody noticed the damage being done, it was still there and it made every waking second of Doris' life a constant reminder that she would never have what the two boys did.

Everything was so perfect until alcohol consumed the man she loved more than life itself. It stole him and handed back in return an ugly, selfish, evil monster. That monster ripped Doris' life to shreds, and did almost the same thing to her body. But she couldn't run away. Not because she could still see even the tiniest ounce of goodness left in that... that creature. No. It was because she had nowhere to run to. Nowhere to run to but her mind. Her mind that stored all of the wonderful memories from a time that seemed to be a million years ago now.

Doris shuffled out of her kitchen as the sound of laughter subsided from the two boys next door. She passed by what used to be her shared room with her husband and sighed. She sleeps on the coach now. Doris peers into the room where John is lying unconscious on the messy, unmade bed, cans littered around the small room, clothes filthy, hair full of dirt and grease, a smug grin plastered on his face, and Doris couldn't look anymore!

She made her way into the sitting room where she pulled out the only video tape she still owned. The video of their first dance. She pushed it into the player and watched the dusty screen start to glow before emitting a fuzzy image. There's a blushing bride in a beautiful long, white gown, pink and white flowers in her hair. Her handsome groom has an arm around her waist and is wearing a dashing tux. A crowd of people gather around the couple and watch on with happy faces as the couple sway to the soft melody of the music. The bride lets out a laugh of pure joy and happiness.

Doris stares at the image on screen with silent tears slipping down her face. Why did it all change?

Room 25B

17:03

Zoe was sat cross-legged on the floor of her bedroom with her ear pressed up against the wall, desperately trying to hear what was going on in the flat next to hers. Everyone had always said she was far too noisy, she preferred the term curious. It made her sound more adventurous and less creepy.

Zoe shut her eyes in attempt to strengthen her sense of hearing. All of a sudden a black ball of fluff entered the room and pounced onto her lap.

"Kiki!" She sighed looking down at her cat.

"I`m trying to listen to the Trainers, they're so cute together!" She explained to the cat who clearly had no interest.

Kiki just stared back with a blank look on her face before running out the door again.

"Yeah well what would you know?!" Zoe argued even though Kiki wasn`t in the least bit bothered.

She leaned closer towards the once a white wall that was now plastered with various drawing and posters. The faint sound of music and a woman laughing softly bounced against the concrete wall.

"Oh my God they are so cute together" Zoe awed as she picked herself up off the floor. She stood up and brushed the black fur that her "flat-mate" had left on her clothes. It wasn`t like they were anything fancy, just an old band shirt and some charity shop jeans, which on further inspection, were for men. She had been unemployed for quite a while, so new clothes weren`t the priority.

Zoe took two steps back before flopping backwards onto her bed that was cluttered with even more drawings, but they weren`t wall worthy. Moving her failed attempts aside, she uncovered her laptop from beneath the mountains of paper. The bright glow of the screen was blinding in the poorly lit room. It took a couple of moments for Zoe`s eyes to adjust and when they did, she didn`t believe them.

She had an e-mail. Do people even email each other anymore? Shrugging, she clicked on the red square that hovered over the white envelope and waited for the message to load. When it did Zoe was certain that her eyes were deceiving her this time. It wasn`t your usual "Congratulations you`ve won! Just send us your bank details and you will receive your triceratops in the post!" No. It was an actual, genuine email. Never mind that, it was an actual genuine email, about a job.

Zoe leapt off her bed in a frenzy of shock and excitement.

"I GOT A JOB!" she shrieked, earning a displeased meow from Kiki in the other room. Zoe suddenly froze on the spot and starred off into the distance as if she was having an epiphany.

"MOM!"

She knew she was forgetting something. Quickly she got to work again searching through the mess on her bed.

As she felt her hand grip around the plastic casing of her phone she grabbed it and pulled it off of the bed.

"AHA!" she announced triumphantly.

Zoe`s hands were shaking as she scrolled through the contacts on her phone until she reached the one that read "Mom". She clicked the bright, green call button and bit her lip. She hopped from toe to toe in excitement her Mom was going to be so proud!

Apparently Zoe couldn't have been more wrong. Her mother wasn`t impressed at all, in fact she laughed at the fact that Zoe would even consider a job in "just some shop". She ended up hanging up in the middle of one of her mothers' famous lectures.

She couldn`t handle it. Her Mom had this crazy misconception that everyone and anyone could get a big job in a fancy company. It was extremely frustrating to try and try again, and then when it finally pays off your own mother is still not proud.

Sighing, Zoe went to her contacts once again in search of a better reaction this time. She finally arrived at her best friend, Brendon, and pressed the call button once again. She took a breath and pushed all the negative things her mother had said to the back of her mind, as usual. Once she heard the phone being picked up she wasted no time in sharing the good news with someone who actually cared.

"Guess got a job? ME!" Zoe screamed down the phone to a slightly shocked, but happy Brendon. Why couldn`t her Mom be this proud?

Room 24B

17:28

Dan was sat in his bathtub in just his underwear when he heard the girl next door scream, although he couldn`t bring himself to care about what it was that she was so happy about. Not in that way of "oh I don`t care about anyone, I hate everyone!" it was more like "I`m a full-grown man sitting in my bath covered in self-inflicted injuries, I`m a little distracted".

Dan stared down at his body and he felt the guilt begin to rise up inside him. The voices in his head screamed out "FAILURE", and as usual he believed them.

He had been doing this for years, yet every time he dragged a blade across his skin he felt immediate guilt for what he had done. It`s not like he wanted to do it, God no! But the sad and simple fact was that it worked. For a few moments Dan was in control. However, this was usually very short-lived and soon enough the weight of the world was crushing him like a ton of bricks once again, only this time it was even heavier than before.

Every single time it became harder and harder to feel something. Every single time Dan had to go deeper and deeper.

Every single time he got uglier and uglier.

And every single time he needed it more and more.

It was Dan's dirty little secret. His way of escaping all the problems he had made up in his own head. He was fully aware of how crazy it sounded to someone who hadn`t been through it. He didn`t even understand it himself. All he knew was that it helped. Even if the relief was only temporary, it helped, and he wasn`t planning on giving up anytime soon.

Sighing, Dan got up on shaky legs. He clung to the wall for support as he stepped slowly out of the tub and sat himself on the floor. He reached to his left and pulled out the first aid-kit he kept in the small press beside the toilet. It had become a routine at this stage:

Become sad/anxious over something stupid and unimportant

Feel the need to cut

Supress the urges and tell yourself they`ll leave

They don`t

Cut

Feel guilty

Get cleaned up and try to forget about it

Promise it won`t happen again

And repeat

Sticking to the routine that seemed to rule his life Dan cleaned the fresh cuts on his stomach and thighs. He hissed the damp cloth made contact with his damaged skin. Soon enough he was all done and bandaged up, but he was still feeling as if he needed more.

This was getting more difficult every day.

Dan got up quickly to clean up the mess he had left in the bath, too quickly. His head began to spin and his legs became weak. Before he knew it Dan was lying in a crumpled mess on the cold, hard floor of the bathroom. His entire body ached and his brain screamed abuse at him.

He made no effort to get up what so ever. What was the point? He just curled up even more and lay there trying to shut up his mind.

Dan's` entire body began shaking and tears filled his eyes. Shaking turned into crying and crying turned into sobbing. Loud, ugly, sobs that tore through his chest and ripped his throat to shreds. It was a heartbreaking sight, but it`s not like anyone could see it anyway.

Sometimes Dan wished someone would find out. That they`d come along and they`d save him. He could tell them what was going on and they`d care. They`d sit with him and comfort him when he was at his worst. And they`d tell him he was worth so much more. But then he remember how selfish that was, and that no one would want to hear about his problems, nobody would care, nobody would come along and hold his hand, because he wasn`t worth it. Dan lay there as his sobs grew louder and louder wishing he was someone else.

Room 23B

17:47

"Turn down dat noise for a sec would ya!" Patricia complained to her friend, Angel. Ironic, that she would be called Angel and not give a damn about anyone but herself. Still, Patricia had been her best friend since playschool, just like their Mas were, and their Mas were…

"Excuse you? `Dis is quality music!" Angel argued over the blaring music that was pouring out of the hot pink radio that was sitting on the nightstand.

"Whatever just shut your face for one minute, Jesus, it`s not dat hard!" Patricia shot back.

"I think your man next door is cryin`or somethin," she said quickly moving towards the wall, turning off the radio as she went.

"Hey!" Angel whined. Trish sent a glare her way and she shut up. Sighing, she lifted herself off the bed where she had been lying and made her way over to Patricia by the wall.

"Ha! You`re right. He`s ballin` his little eyes out!" Angel laughed.

"It`s not funny! God knows what`s wrong with de poor bloke. I seen him in de lift a few times and he just looked so sad," Patricia explained, her voice getting quieter towards the end. She knew exactly how horrible it was and how much worse other people could make it just because they didn`t understand or even care.

The noise soon stopped and Angel jumped backwards to land on the bed once again.

"Can`t believe I just missed dat song `cause you fancy de pants off dat little emo. Like Jesus, Trish it`s so feckin` obvious," Angel mumbled, rolling her eyes. Did her best friend really want to go out with that?

"First off I DON`T fancy him, I don`t even know him! More important, could ya not care about anyone but yourself for ONCE? For de love of Jeazus, de poor fella could be writin` his suicide note for all we know!" Patricia screamed, maybe she was being a bit over-dramatic but it`s not like Angel would have cared anyway.

"Dats not my problem Trish, if ya wanta make it yours den fair fecks to ya but don`t get me involved. I`ve already got me own stuff ta deal with, I don`t need his feckin`"issues" as well!" Seriously, what the hell was wrong with Trish? She didn`t even know the guy.

"You're a wagon you are! You don`t give two shits about anyone but yourself and I'm sick of dealin`with your crap all de time! Get lost, I don`t wanta see ya right now," Patricia fought back.

"Get out of me house I said! No joke I`m actually goin`ta swing for ya in a minute if you don`t leave!" she warned Angel. She was so angry! How could anyone be so selfish? Angel stood up and pressed her forehead against Patricia's.

"Wha? You`ve got some neck on ya thinkin`ya can speak to me like dat. I`ll leave, but if ya think I'm comin` back ya must be as feckin` mental as he is!" Angel spat at Patricia before making her way to the door. Patricia followed behind, becoming angrier with every step. Angel swung open the door and stepped out.

"Have fun slittin` your wrists with dat saddo, ya little bitch!" Angel hissed before turning around and stomping down the hall towards the lift.

"Oh just feck off with yourself!" Patricia yelled before slamming the door shut.

Room 22B
18:06

"Yikes!" Cade chuckled to himself as he heard the two girls screaming their heads off. They were forever fighting with each other, yet no matter how many times they were "so not friends anymore", they always made up within the same week. Cade found it hilarious. They couldn't stand one another but they could barely function properly without the other.

"Well then feck you!" Cade heard, followed by an eruption of laughter. However, it wasn`t from the girls next door, so who was it?

"Ah crap." Cade sighed as he realised whose voice it was. He abandoned the dishes he was cleaning and left the kitchen.

Cade practiced his cross face as he marched towards the play-room on the other side of the flat. He flung open the bright green door to find his kids rolling around the floor in hysterical laughter.

"What do you two think you`re doing!" Cade bellowed, trying to sound assertive and failing miserably.

"Come on Da! Don`t be a bitch," Sage told her father with a smug grin on her face.

"Young lady! That language is unacceptable in this house. Apologise immediately!" Cade said sternly.

She was ten years old for God sake! This did nothing but make her laugh even more. Before he could even get another word in, he was interrupted again.

"Sage isn`t a lady! I saw her picking her nose earlier!" her younger brother, Blake, protested. "I wasn`t picking it was scratching it from the inside, you idiot!" Sage complained rolling her eyes.

"DA! Sage called me an idiot. I`m not an idiot! I got all my spellings right and…" Blake began to fight back until Cade stopped them.

"That`s it. Family meeting NOW!" he shouted.

After some intense negotiations gathered around a poorly con-structed IKEA table, an agreement was met.

If Sage swore again, no cartoons for an entire week!

However, Cade wasn`t that cruel, so it was also agreed that if both Blake and Sage pinky-promised not argue for the rest of the day, they would have pancakes for dinner.

Cade left the room with a smile on his face. "Top class parenting!" he complimented himself as he returned to the kitchen.

"Let me be the judge of that." Cade turned around to see his wife, Jade, throwing her jacket onto the coach before also moving into the kitchen.

"I`ll have you know I just put Supernanny to shame." he announced proudly.

"I`m sure you did." Jade said before giving him a quick peck on the cheek.

"Plans for dinner?" she asked as she hopped up and sat on the counter.

"My famous pancakes!" Cade answered with a dramatic hair flip.

"Cool." Jade smiled. "Do ya wanna let the kids help?" she questioned.

"Sure! You go get them, I`ll get the ingredients." Cade told her.

"Do you guys wanna make some pancakes?" Jade called down the hall.

"You feckin` bet!"

"Oh no"

Hallway

18:33

Kate hopped from foot to foot impatiently as she waited for the lift doors to open. She had literally run out the door from work. Her short, black hair was windswept and her eye make-up was half way down her face at this stage. She had so much to organize in so little time! The lift in her apartment block reminded her of her boss. It was old, slow, didn`t do its job properly and smelt kind of weird.

"At least he gave you the weekend off," she told herself as the doors slowly creaked open. Kate stepped out of the lift and into the familiar corridor, lifting her backpack higher up onto her shoulder as she began spped-walking towards her flat. As she passed her neighbours in 22B, Kate heard the kids laughing and their mother screaming in horror. She knew the family quite well and was good friends with the similarly named couple. They were great people, if not a bit odd. Kate would even babysit from time to time. However, work had been pretty hectic lately, so she hadn`t seen them as much anymore. She would have called in for a cup of tea and a chat if she didn`t have so much to get done in the next half an hour.

HALF AN HOUR!

Kate realised just how far behind schedule she was when she caught a glance of her watch. Abandoning all thoughts of the friendly family, she raced towards her apartment. Dropping her bag on the ground in front of the door and pulling out her key, she jammed it into the lock. Then Kate heard a terrible noise.

SNAP

Yanking the key out of the lock, she discovered it had broken in half. Leaving her stranded outside her apartment with only,

She checked her watch,

27 minutes!!!

"OH FOR THE LOVE OF......

Room 27B

18:45

Jamie and Matthew were curled up under a blanket on the sofa, watching some anime that according to Matt was "the greatest thing to ever be animated by mere mortals."

Jamie didn`t really get it, and the fact that Matt insisted on watching it subbed and not dubbed made it even worse. At the moment though, he honestly couldn't care. He was just happy to see that his boyfriend had recovered from what had happened. He would have watched paint dry if he had to. The sounds of a woman shouting tore Jamie out of his daydream. Blinking fast and rubbing his eyes he looked over at Matthew who had his eyes practically glued to the screen.

"Hey, Matt did you hear something?" Jamie asked with a yawn.

"Shhh, not now!" Matthew shushed.

"Seriously pause that for a second, I can hear something."

"The only thing I can hear is you talking over my show!"

"Ugh, how do you even know what's going on?"

"Have you not been paying any attention?"

"No."

"I hate you."

"Love you."

"Bitch!"

"Loser."

The Bingo Bus
Tom Knightly

Dublin, 1982

Dan hated driving the "eld ones" to bingo. All they did was gossip and natter. Dan hated gossip. He hated the idea of someone sticking their noses in other people's business. Although he hated being called 'Dan The Man With a Van' even more. He pulled up outside Mrs. McDunnagh's house. She was waiting on the curb as always.

"You're 7 minutes late, Mr. Murphy," she said.

"Afternoon, Mrs. Dunnagh." She hated being called that.

Dan smirked to himself before closing the door and driving off. Even though she was a miserable old woman, Dan liked her. She wasn't like the rest of them. While the rest nattered and gossiped about things that weren't any of their concern, she just sat there with her nose buried in a book. Eventually they arrived at The Grand Bonnaue Casino. Even though it was called "grand" it was really far from it. It looked like a large grey block that blended in with the other bleak surrounding buildings. There was a few windows on the second floor of the building but for some reason they were all blacked out. Just above these windows was a huge red sign, which read "th Gra d Cas o". Most of the letters had fallen away over time and Bonnaue had obviously neglected to repair them.

"Righ' ladies, off ya get!" ordered Dan.

All the old ladies hobbled off the bus, one by one, onto the grey path. The last one off was Mrs. McDunnagh.

"Thank you, Dan," said Mrs. McDunnagh.

Dan had been pretty a taken aback by this. She had never said anything positive to Dan. He felt he should do something nice in return, like say "you're welcome" or help her with her massive handbag, but all he could manage was "See ya later, Dunnagh". Then he closed the doors and drove off towards the pub. The pub wasn't far from the casino. The outside of the pub was very normal, apart from the name John Paul's. As he walked into the pub the first thing he noticed was the large amount of figurines of saints and paintings of the sacred heart, but the most noticeable thing in this room was the huge picture of the owner of this fine establishment shaking hands with the Pope John Paul.

"Ah here he is, Dan The Man with th—"

"Finish that sentence and I'll break your bloody nose!" Dan knew the sound of that annoying voice. It was the voice of the owner of this pub, Mikey McCabe.

"Now, now Dan, there's no need for dat," Mickey said with obvious fear in his voice.

"Well ge' me a sodding drink and maybe I'll le' ya off," replied Dan.

"Wh… What will it be?"

"Cider."

As Mikey pulled Dan his pint, Dan dropped into a stool at the bar. It creaked as he sat down, as if it was groaning under his huge weight. Mikey set the pint in front of Dan. Dan snatched it off the bar top and took a big mouthful and grimaced.

"This tastes like piss!"

"Wha-"

"It's bloody warm."

"Oh that would've been the power ou'age this morning. It's only jus' back on."

Dan grunted and finished his pint. Then he asked for another. He knew he would be over the limit but he didn't care. He had worked with all the Guards in the area. This pint was a little better but it wasn't cold. Dan quickly finished his pint and paid, leaving the money on the counter and stood up to leave. The stool creaked again but this time it sounded as if it was a sigh of relief.

He arrived outside the casino a few minutes later. He was a bit early, so he waited until the eld ones began to file into the bus, still nattering away. As they piled in, Dan noticed that McDunnagh's seat was empty. He found this odd because she was usually very punctual. When she eventually did arrived she seemed to be having trouble carrying her bag. Dan thought he should try to do something considering she had been so nice to him. He decided the polite thing to do would be to help her carry her huge yellow handbag. This single act of kindness would be McDunnagh's only fault in her flawless plot.

"Let me give ya a hand wit' dat."

Before she could reply, Dan had grabbed the bag off her.

"Jaysus Dunnagh! Wh' do ya have in 'ere?" Dan said as he reached into her bag.

"No don't—" Before she had a chance to stop him, he had opened her bag. He looked back up at her, confused. He looked like he was trying to narrow down the reasons as to why there would be a gun, four large bonds of euros, and a bloodied straight razor in her handbag. Then Dan's expression changed from confused and slightly scared to a cheeky smile.

"Did well at the bingo tonigh' I see," Dan said with the cheeky smile still slapped on his face. "Must be my lucky day," McDunnagh replied with a malicious smile of her own.

"Well you 'better hurry onto the bus 'dere and you can tell us all about it."

"I'd rather not," McDunnagh said, her smile retreating from her face. She then snatched the bag back off Dan and hurried up the stairs of the bus. Dan grabbed her arm and whispered to her, "Tell me or ya can tell 'de Guards". Dan let go of her arm and lumbered into his seat. Thoughts were flying through his mind. He didn't even notice that he was dropping the eld ones off. McDunnagh just sat in her seat staring at the back of Dan's head, tapping her foot nervously. He purposely dropped her off last.

"Thank-you," she said, as she was about to leave.

"Are ya not gonna invite us in?"

"No," she replied bluntly. Just as she was about to get off, the door slammed shut.

"I think I might have said dat like it was a genuine question," Dan said with his hand on the door controls.

"I meant of course, Dan. Please do come in," McDunnagh said through gritted teeth.

"Great. I'm dying for a cuppa. Here, let me help ya with dat big eld bag o' yours," Dan snatched the bag out of her hands. When McDunnagh unlocked her front door, Dan charged past her with the yellow handbag in his grip.

The hallway was very bare and old fashioned. The floors were left uncarpeted to reveal the bare varnished floorboards. The only pieces of furniture in the entire hallway were a small table and a large gilt mirror. The table sat below the mirror to the left of the doorway. It was scarred from age but obviously sturdy. The mirror was far more intriguing. It was a rather large ovate mirror about three feet in diameter. The frame was beautifully hand-carved and reminded Dan of waves at the pinacle of their height. The mirror itself though was not so beautiful. It was completely cracked as if something was thrown into it.

Dan walked pass this into the kitchen. The kitchen was also very plain and antiquated. The sink and stove were in the left-hand corner of the room. A small, unbecoming plastic table stood beside a window to the right of the room. Only one chair sat at it, facing the window. Suddenly Dan heard a squawk come from his right. He stepped into the kitchen to find a large, brass birdcage. Onside there was a huge luminous green parrot that sat on a shelf.

"Heil Hitler!" it squawked at Dan. Dan chuckled to himself. He found a small wooden chair beside the cage. He pulled it up to the table and sat down.

"Ya gunna make us dat cuppa tea?" he asked. McDunnagh stood in the doorway of the kitchen, sneering at Dan, but knowing he had the upper hand, she reluctantly went over to the kettle and made tea. She sat the two mugs down on the kitchen table with such force that Dan jumped. Then he took a large mouthful of the tea.

"Now back to the business at hand," he said.

"And what would that be?" asked McDunnagh.

"Oh you know the fact you've a gun, lots more money than I'd earn in 2 years and this yoke," Dan said as he pulled out the bloodied straight razor, but held it at arms length. "Whose blood is this?"

"Bonnaue's..."

"The bloke who owns the casino?"

"Owned."

"Owned then, and why did ya kill him?"

"I never said I killed him.."

"So ya didn' kill him?"

"I never said that either…"

"For the love of Christ!" Dan said, as he put his hands on his head.

"If you knew what he did you'd have no sympathy for that bastard."

"Then tell me."

"When I was younger I lived in occupied France. I lived just outside of Paris when the Germans came in with their tanks. I was dammed if I was going to give up my country so easily. So me and David joined the Resistance…"

"Who's David?" Dan interrupted.

"He was my husband."

"How come he wasn't conscripted?"

"He had a bad back from when a train rail fell on him. Now do you want to hear my sodding story or what?!"

"Please do continue, Dunnagh."

"He was a train conductor so since he couldn't do any actual fighting. He told the Resistance what train was coming in and when it was coming. My job was to plant bombs on railways with a demolitions expert, which was Bonnaue. He eventually sold me and David out, for roughly the same amount of money in that bag. Plus interest. That straight razor is the only thing I have left of David. Thought it would be fitting to kill him with that."

"Sounds like he had it coming."

"Its not something to be proud of, Dan."

"On the contrary, Dunnagh, which I'm sure isn't your real name, I've got me own sob story," Dan said as he raised his mug to his lips, taking a long slurp of the tea.

"So are you going to tell me this sob story of yours?" she asked, impatience in her voice. Without pausing from his tea Dan lifted his index finger into the air, while he drained the rest of his cup.

"Right, back in 'de day, I was a Guard. Not just 'dat but an inspector. Nothing too remarkable abou' me 'cept that I got the job done".

"What happened to you?"

"The drink got to me," he said with a deep sigh. "I was given a case about a missing person. Now this person was a sort of childhood friend of mine, so I dedicated myself to finding her..."

"What was her name?"

"And no matter where I wen' I could find nothing," Dan said, obviously ignoring the question. "But I knew who it was..."

"Who?"

"But I couldn't get enough evidence to convict," Dan said, again ignoring the question. "They all told me to leave it, said 'she was gone' and that I should 'just move on'. I couldn' though. I just couldn'. It just sat at the bottom of me gut, all day, every day.

"Drink seemed to be the only thing that made me forget… so that's how everything fell apar'. Drinking at work, becoming 'aggressive and reckless' and that's why people are scared of me. It's why I now drive a bus full of eld ladies to bingo."

"I'm sorry…"

"Ahh, hardly your fault. Well dere's my sob story, you best be ready to go soon."

"Go? Go where?"

"Anywhere that's not this country! I assume you don' wan' to be done for murder."

It took McDunnagh a while to get a suitcase ready but when she came down, suitcase and parrot cage in hand, she found Dan leaning against the front door picking at his nails.

"Why are you doing this?" she asked. "You're supposed to be an ex-Guard."

"Why I'm helpin' ya? Well, once a wise man said 'an eye for an eye makes 'de whole world blind' bu' both you and me know differn'. We know 'dats not de way de world work on small scale, so wha' im doing here is called helpin' ou' a fellow philosopher."

Sweet Innocence
Adam Lyons

It's a busy, dark morning in Los Angeles:

"Come on,"

Andrew Kennedy punches the horn aggressively and yells out the window. He jerks the car forward. Ah shit! Andrew slowly emerges out of the car and walks over to the car in front.

"Hi, I'm sorry about the damage!" he says to the person behind the blacked out windows. The car door opens and a man in his 20's hops out.

"It's cool, do you have insurance?" says the 20 year old, "my name is Jonathan."

"I do, I'll get the details, and they should be in my car." Andrew shuffles through the glove box and comes out with his papers.

"I'll ring them and my buddy who is a mechanic."

After ten minutes, Jonathan's friend turns up and assesses the damage to both cars.

"Well, Andrew it just needs a bit of paint, Jonathan your car is worse; it needs a new back panel which is about $1000. Your insurance will cover it though."

"Alright, thanks, I'll be on to you later," says Jonathan relieved.

"Now that it is sorted I believe we are done here?" Jonathan says to Andrew in a rush and slowly walking to his car.

"Yes we are," replies Andrew.

As Jonathan drives off, he rings his boss.

"You have reached the ATNT voicemail messages of 3234876510, please leave a message after the beep"

"Michael, its Jonathan here, sorry I'm late, I was in a bit of a car crash, I'll be in, in about twenty minutes."

Twenty-five minutes later, Jonathan arrives outside work and walks in the front door.

"Morning Tom" says Jonathan to the door guard who was sitting with his head down.

With no answer Jonathan tries again, this time walking over to Tom. As he does, he sees blood under the table coming from Tom. He slowly retreats to the door as he hears shouting and gun shots. Terrified he runs to the car park, checking that the robbers didn't see him. He fumbles for the keys in his pocket as he dials 911.

"Hello 911, how can I help?"

"There is someone dead and I believe the gun men are still in the building."

"Where are you?"

"I'm at L.A Banking, West 23rd Street."

"Okay, police and an ambulance are on route. Stay put!"

After waiting a while:

Jonathan panics; he gets out of the car and slowly approaches the building. He looks through the window in to the offices. He sees all his work mates in a group except his boss Michael. He scans the room for anyone else who might be injured or dead. He sees no one. As he approaches the door he can hear the sirens of a police car in the distance. He doesn't know whether to pull Tom's body out or leave it in the place he was shot in. He opens the door with ease and tries not to make a noise. He decides to check Tom for a pulse. There isn't any. Jonathan tries to remember what he learned in first aid training that the company made him study. As he sits trying to remember, he hears more shouting but this time it is closer. He can hear the sirens getting nearer now. He runs for the door to tell the police. As he makes a movement to the door a bullet whistles pass him and stops. One of the gun men yells,

"Another person, another person."

Jonathan makes a burst for the door. The police cars screech around the corner as the gun men let loose at them. Jonathan jumps behind them for safety just missing the bullets.

***

As the doorbell echoed in the house, Stacey opens the door.

"Hello, Mrs McAlester?"

"Yes, who are you?"

"I'm Sergeant Cook and this is my colleague, could we come in for a few minutes?"

"Yes of course., says Stacey worried.

As she lets them into in the hall she points to the sitting room,

"Can I offer you any tea or coffee?"

"No ma'am, no thank you." He looks towards the sitting room door and back to her.

"Ma'am, I'm afraid we have some bad news, do you mind sitting down?"

She sits only wondering what the bad news could be.

"Ma'am, I'm afraid to tell you your husband was shot dead in work today." Mr Cook says to her in a fragile voice.

Shocked, just sitting there sadness on her face, her mouth opens but no sound is coming out. As it starts to hit her she cries out but does not says a word. Mr Cook sits there with his colleague also not saying a word. After five minutes of crying she stops and says "Thank you for coming and telling me, if you don't mind I've to go pick my children from school?"

"That is fine, here is my card if you need anything," as he stands up. Mr Cook heads for the door; Stacey walks them to it and closes it firmly behind them. She waits a few minutes before leaving. She gets in her car. She reverses the car out the driveway. As she is driving she thinks back on the memories she had with her husband.

As she pulls up to the school she sees her children happy and full of life. She knows what she was going to say would hurt them. When they get in the car she asks how their day was and all those questions. She thinks of any reason to go to 'Toys 'R' Us.'

"What time is daddy going to be home at?" asks Ellie the youngest daughter.

"I don't know, honey."

"I can't wait to show him my new Barbie doll."

"I'm sure he will love it," sighing to herself.

When they get home, Stacey brings Ellie, Tom Jr and Jessie in to the sitting room and tells them the bad news.

"Daddy just rang me there, he said he won't be coming back; he has gone a world trip with work. He said he loves the three of you," she says to the children who are looking lost.

"I've to find a job," she thinks to herself.

***

"So, what makes you fit to become a secretary in my company?" shouts a cocky man called James Nolan, a local businessman known to be interested in legal and illegal business.

"Well Mr Nolan, I was a secretary for many years before I met my husband, I have worked in schools, prisons and in the airport," Stacey says very nervously.

"That's very good but nothing like working for my business," says James laughing.

"Look Mr Nolan, I need this, my husband was shot dead. I have no money coming in," begs Stacey.

"You can work a week and I want to see how that goes, you will be paid half wage till I see if your fit enough to work in my company. Is that okay?"

"Thank you so much, when do I start?" says Stacey excitedly.

"Now! Get me a coffee, two sugars and milk."

Stacy, overjoyed that he said yes, gets up, shakes hands with James and walks to the coffee shop. She orders the coffee and grabs the sugar before starting to heads back to office. She starts to walk up the stairs, when she hears a scream. She runs over to a window. She sees a child getting blindfolded and put in a van.

"What is happening?" she wonders.

One of the men punches the child and yells "Shut up!"

She gets her phone out and takes a picture and ducks under the window. She then dials LAPD.

"LAPD, how can we be of service?"

"Hello, there is a kidnapping in progress; I can't get to the girl because there is no door in to the garage!"

"What street are you on?"

"The offices are on Hill Street."

"Whose offices are you in?"

"I'm in James Nolan's offices."

"Okay, there are officers on route. Try not to be noticed, he is known for kidnapping children." Nervously, she hangs up and walks outside into the air.

***

"Where is she with my coffee?!" says James sitting there impatiently.

"Oh, shit the cops, get out of here everybody," yells James running for the door, leaving everything. He makes a beeline straight to the door. He runs down the stairs skipping every second step. As he reaches the door to the street the police kick it in, catching him in the face and then they arrest him.

Thirty minutes later....

"Are you the lady that called the police?" asks an officer to Stacey.

"Yes I am why?"

"There was money on getting evidence on this man. You've just received $100,000 and one of his cars, the Lamborghini Veneno, if you would like it."

"$100,000 and the car are you serious?" said Stacey about to cry with happiness.

"Yes, the money will be wired to your account in a week."

***

"Order in the court," yells the Judge, hitting his, gavel off the table.

The room went quiet.

"We will hear from the prosecutor first," shouts the Judge

"Thank you, your Honour. What I would like to do first is, call Stacey McAlester."

Stacey gets up and slowly walks to the podium.

"Good morning, Mrs McAlester," says the prosecutor

"Good morning, Sir."

"Now firstly, I would like to ask your connection to Mr Nolan."

"Em, I was his secretary. I had started that day," Stacey says worried. "Did you see anything suspicious before you went to get him a coffee?"

"No. I didn't see anything like that at all.""Okay and what about when you had returned to the building?" the prosecutor says wondering.

"Well, I saw a girl getting blindfolded. Then a man punched her. Then the same man threw her into the van."

Noise comes from the back of the room by people in shock.

"Order!" yells the Judge.

"Do you have proof of this?" asks the prosecutor.

"Yes Sir, I do have proof. It's a picture I took on my phone," says Staccy.

The picture gets projected on a screen. The picture is the two tall, white skinned men. One is holding the girl while the other is putting a blindfold on her. There is a white long van behind them.

"Thank you, Stacey, you may take your seat again," Stacey gets up and walks back to her seat.

"People of the Jury, the next part of evidence we got out of Mr Nolan's office are the files that he has signed."

The prosecutor picks up some of the sheets and gives it to someone in the jury. They pass it around all examining it in their own way.

"Thank you, your honour, I rest my case."

"The defendant may now say their case," yells the judge.

"Your Honour, the defendant would like to admit to all this if a deal may be made," says James' lawyer.

"Prosecutor, what do you believe of this?" asks the judge.

"Your Honour, we would allow a deal if he gets a minimum forty-five years," after thinking for a few seconds

"Defendant?" asks the judge.

James and his lawyer talk for a few seconds. After talking about it the lawyer says,

"The defendant would agree."

More chatter comes from the back of the room ending again with the judge yelling for order.

"Jury you may make your decision."

After two hours of talking the jury comes out of the room with their decision"

"Jury, have you made your decision?" bellows the Judge.

"Yes, your Honour, we have," replies the foreman

"Well, can you tell us, foreman?"

"We find Mr Nolan," with a pause, the foreman finishes, "Guilty of sixteen cases of children trafficking, smuggling an unknown amount of cocaine and other substances into Los Angeles as well as firearms and exotic animals."

Gasps and cheers come from the back of the room as the foreman finishes.

"Thank you jury for your deliberation"

After a few minutes the judge asks "May the defendant please stand."

"Mr James Nolan, you have been proven guilty of sixteen cases of children trafficking, smuggling cocaine and other substances into Los Angeles as well as smuggling fire arms and exotic animals. You will serve a time of fifty-two years in jail," orders the judge.

***

The gate opens with a buzz.

"Welcome to the king suite Mr Nolan" said a guard laughing. The rest of the inmates start screaming. "Your cellmate will be Carlos Rodríguez," the guard says to James getting thrown in to the cell.

"Hola, buenas días," said a shadow in the corner of the cell.

"You must be Carlos."

"Sí, Mister Nolan, ¿Qué tal?" says Carlos.

"Bien. And you?" replies James thinking.

"Muy bien, why you here?" Carlos says trying to speak English.

"Long story. Can you not speak English?"

"Yes but not not well," says Carlos

"Why are you in an American prison than your own, you foreign?"

"I was caught doing crime here, you rude cabrón," says Carlos aggressively.

"Guard can we get a bloody translator in here!" says James laughing.

"No, Nolan, you've only to deal with Rodriguez for another three days and he is getting released," says the floor guard.

"So you are getting out in three days, are you?"

"Sí, you cabrón," says Carlos and spits at the floor near James.

Three days later:

"Here are your clothes, a watch, a wallet, $40, pictures and your phone," says the warden to Carlos.

"Muchas gracias, señor."

Carlos walks out the door, a car drives by blasting 'The Chain' by Fleetwood Mac. He takes in the sun and starts to walk down the street, until he comes upon a Taco Bell. He walks into the restaurant, buys a taco and a bottle of coke.

"Ah, never taste so good," after he eats the taco. He takes out his phone goes to the contacts page and clicks on Padre.

It rings until a man answered

"¿Dígame?"

"Hola, Padre, ¿Qué tal?" The phone beeps,

"¿Padre? ¿Padre? Cabrón,"

He continues down the contact list, he clicks on Pablo.

"Hola?"

"Hola Pablo, ¿Qué tal?

"Who this?" asks Pablo

"It is Carlos."

"You released today?" says Pablo wondering.

"Sí."

"Jesús, you in time for our next job."

"No! No!"

"Sí, you doing robbery!"

"No, Pablo, just out, I jail, not tú."

Pablo hangs up and Carlos aggressively walks down the street kicking a stone.

***

He heads towards his friends house, Isabela. He knocks softly on the door. A woman opens the door "Carlos?"

"Hola Isabela."

"¡Tú carbón!"She says slamming the door in his face.

"Isabela, open door," cries Carlos

"No, go, you ruin life," she says in a sad voice.

He walks away sadly. He takes his phone out and dials Pablo's number.

"We need talk!"

"Sí, Little Spain West 3rd Street at 2 o'clock," replies Pablo.

Carlos looks at his watch, 2:30,

"Where is he?" wonders Carlos.

"Do you want anything else, sir?" asks a waiter.

"Sí, Club Limón."

"Okay, I will bring it over, it's on the man over there," pointing to a man wearing sunglasses and a hat. The man gets up and walks to Carlos' table.

"Hola Carlos," said the man.

"Bunas días, Pablo," replies Carlos.

"Nice meet you"

"Just give facts to me!" says Carlos fed up.

"Fine, car robbery-" he is interrupted by the bartender brings the drinks over,

"Here is Club Lemon."

"Gracias."

"As I was saying, car robbery, a Lambarghini Veneno, silver, worth $5,300,000. The second car is an Audi Le Mans Concept worth $5,000,000 and finally Ferrari P4 worth $4,800,000"

As he adds up the numbers in his head he realises and almost shouts "$15,600,000, are you kidding?" gulping his drink.

"I am not; all owned by James Nolan, there is one problem the Veneno has gone to some woman, so have to get that separately."

"The one just arrested?"

"Sí, we all get $3, 120,000."

"I can't"

"What? Why?"

"I just in jail with him, he was a cabrón."

"Does that not want you want to rob them even more?"

"Kinda, I need think it over, I text you later," Carlos stands up, finishes his drink and walks off.

Carlos walks around for the rest of the day

"Should I rob cars, my family don't want to talk with me, if I go back to jail they will hate me more but if I had the money I would be able to survive again," thought Carlos. Carlos takes out his phone and dials Pablo's number.

"Sorry you don't have enough credit to make this call," said the phone. Carlos aggressively hangs up and mutters under his breath. He walks over to a Payphone after searching for one and puts the money in the machine; he dials Pablo's number again.

"¿Hola?" asks Pablo lost.

"Hola Pablo," replies Carlos.

"O, Carlos ¿Qué?"

"I want more details before I decide if I do job."

"What want to know?" thinks Pablo.

"How many people?"

"Cinco including you and me."

"Where cars?" asks Carlos suspiciously.

"Veneno is with a lady, others at house."

"What day, time and date?" wonders Carlos?

"Monday 16th March, we meet at eight at night."

"Where?"

"23rd Street near L.A Banking."

"I've one last question, who are other three people?"

"There a guy called Andrew Kennedy, who is very aggressive and two brothers Alberto and Adriano."

"Why the American?" Carlos asks suspiciously.

"So we can kinda fit in."

"Okay."

After a minute of thinking Pablo asks,

"What your answer?

"I'm......"

Foedus ad Libertatem
Sadhbh Mac Lochlainn.

November 12th, 2093

It was a dreary Tuesday afternoon. As I pushed my way through the growing hordes of people in the ever busy underground, I sighed at the sheer banality of it all. I was cold and wet and tired and I just wanted to go home but of course the train was delayed and I was stuck on this dreary, overcrowded platform. In an attempted to warm my now completely numb toes I did a little jig in my place, ignoring the funny looks sent in my direction.

I felt my new phone buzzing in my pocket and hastily stopped my jig to answer.

'Hey Mam I'm so sorry I didn't call you sooner I totally forgot. Listen my train's delayed but don't worry I should still be home before dinner... if all goes well. Don't send Peter to pick me up, please. I really don't want to be seen getting into a limo because you know that will just lead to questions and I'm really happy in this school. I don't want to have to move again.'

'W-What... home? No, Alice you mustn't come home... get away while you still can.' I heard my mother gasp over the phone.

'Mom, what's going on? Are you okay, do you want me to call dad?'

'Alistair? Oh no not Alistair he'll kill me he'll kill anyone who knows... Don't trust them, don't believe anything they tell you!' She wailed down the line.

'Mom, calm down, what are you talking about, who's 'they'?'

'They are everyone, your father, the government.'

'You're not making any sense,' I cried

Suddenly my mother's erratic breathing slowed and the rustling in the background went silent. 'Mam… MAM' I screamed terrified.

Just as I was about to hang up and call the fed's her voice came back down the line much calmer then before, that scared me the most.

'I get this feeling sometimes, I feel like I'm being watched, not always, it comes and goes but I can never quite shake it. I used to think I was going crazy but now I know the truth. Don't trust him everything is a lie.'

'Mam I need you to tell me what you mean. I need to understand.'

'It's your father. Find the *Foedus ad libertatem* they will hel-' but before she could utter another word there was a loud bang, a short cry, then silence.

'MAM!' I screamed but the sound was swallowed up by the train finally arriving in the station. As the mass of bodies surged forward towards the open doors I pushed along with them despite my struggle. Suddenly I was shoved to the ground. A searing pain radiated through my head as someone boot connected with my face. Everything went dark.

November 14th, 2093

I regained consciousness slowly, my senses coming back one at a time. It was difficult to even twitch my fingers. I couldn't tell where I was or who was with me. Only one thing was certain. I wasn't in my home.

As I lay on the hard bed, only my thoughts for company, I felt my mind wandering places and dwelling on things that I desperately wanted to suppress. I could vaguely recall my mother's voice telling me something but what, why was she so upset?

Suddenly I dragged out of these thoughts by a sharp cough wrenching itself from my chest. As if a switch had been flicked inside my head: everything that had happened- the phone call, mom, the secrets, it all came back.

Gasping I suddenly found the strength to pull myself up, eyes flying open.

At first all I could see was black and white specks blurring my vision, but after a few second of rapid blinking my vision cleared and I found myself in a sterile hospital room.

I was so busy thinking back on everything that had happened I didn't notice my father until he stepped in front of my line of vision carefully clearing his throat, eyes wary as if I was some wild beast.

We stared at each other for what felt like hours, his eyes wide and cautious. When I narrowed my eyes at him I saw the briefest flash of fear and it was at that moment I knew. Everything my mother had said was true.

Opening my mouth I began to scream nothing in particular at him. But soon I was being pushed down by a flurry of faceless doctors and the world started to go dark again.

November 15th, 2093

When I came around for the second time I made sure to keep my eyes shut and my breathing steady so as not or alert my father or the doctors. I allowed myself to think over the events which had transpired in the underground and then in the hospital.

My father knew what happened to Mam and had known all along. I knew the second I saw that small flicker of fear dart across his eyes that he was somehow involved, I was positive. Mam had told me and he had just confirmed it. What I needed to do now was get out of here and find her, but where exactly was here?

I seemed to be lying on a hard uncomfortable bed – nothing like my bed at home with its soft sheets and plump pillows. My wrists were stuck fast to the side of the bed, when I tried to move them I found that I couldn't, the same went for my ankles. The smell of disinfectant was strong in the air and I winced as it stung my nose. Just behind my head there was a steady rhythmic beeping of machines keeping in time with my heartbeat. The soft sound was relaxing, comforting almost.

I could hear muffled footsteps and whispers just outside my room, so quiet that my steady breathing almost swallowed the sound completely. Apart from that my room was completely silent. I was alone. With this in mind I slowly cracked my eyes open, taking in every detail of the room. My earlier assumption had been correct: I was in a hospital bed. Looking down, I noticed the Velcro straps preventing the movement of my limbs. My father had obviously left and I could see a burly security guard standing outside my closed door. Apart from that, I was alone. The stark room completely empty.

I needed to leave. Now. I had to figure out what was going on. I had never really given it much thought but I was thankful for my slim build as I began to maneuver my wrists under the binding. It took time but eventually I managed to get one hand free. Careful not to disturb any of the wires attached to my body, I moved my arm slowly across myself undoing each strap, carefully easing them off. At one point, I was sure the security guard would realise what I was up to but luckily the moment passed with him stifling a dainty sneeze.

After what felt like days, I finally managed to free myself from the tedious material and I sat silently on the bed, unsure what to do next. If I left now, I couldn't come back but where would I go? I didn't' have anyone anymore, not really. I would have to go out into a world I spent my entire life being sheltered from and find a terrorist organisation. I wanted to run back to Dad, to forget about her and pretend like nothing had happened. I wanted to yell at my mother, to shake her. Why would she tell me to go to *Foedus ad libertatem*, a terrorist group? A group who oppose the government and were the cause of so much death and destruction? They were bad, the *Foedus ad libertatem* were evil, it was how I was raised. How could she, after years and years of telling me how good the government were how they'd helped end the third world war and unite all the countries and remaining populations. How could she then turn to me and tell me to join an organization that was opposed to all of that? The government was good and true and they saved us. They brought us order and unity and peace and control. What the *Foedus ad libertatem* offered us was freedom and freedom led to chaos and chaos led to war.

But if *Foedus ad libertatem* were so bad why had my mother told me to go with them? I needed answers and I knew I couldn't get them from Dad. He had already lied about so much. He was the reason Mam was missing, the reason I was leaving, the reason for God knows what else. No matter how hard I tried I couldn't bring myself to hate him. I don't think I could ever hate the man who had raised me, protected me, loved me. No matter what he did I couldn't hate him. He was my Dad. But as much as I wanted to, I couldn't go back to being the perfect daughter. I needed to find the *Foedus ad libertatem*. They would have the answers.

I gave an experimental tug on the end of one of the wires attached to my arm and when nothing happened, I decided to go one step further, pulling the needle out of my arm completely. This time something happened. The machines behind stopped their steady beeping and began one long ominous note. Lights began to flash. I half expected a robotic voice to sound over the intercom – 'This is not a drill. Repeat. This is not a drill.'- and some screaming nurses to have a meltdown. Instead, the security guard turned and locked eyes with me. He stepped inside my room and ran.

I ripped out the rest of the wires and jump off the bed, towards the window. I was lucky that the fire escape was outside. I would not have made the ten story jump. Steeling my nerve, I stepped outside, stifling my rapidly growing fears before they overcame me. I wasted no time in rushing down the icy steps, gripping the railing and trying not to look down.

As I came to the ninth floor I heard the security guard stepping out onto the fire escape, which creaked ominously under our combined weight. Trying not to think about it I quickened my pace. After another tense minute I reached the bottom and hopped nimbly onto a wall just beneath me. Jumping into the alley, I took off as fast as my legs could carry me. For a moment I was filled with hope. Then there was a thump, followed by the quick pounding of heavy feet behind me.

I urged myself forward, ignoring the stark pain of my bare feet hitting the ground. Despite my efforts, I could hear my captor getting closer, his heavy breath getting louder and louder. I could almost feel it on my neck. I knew he was within reaching distance and I felt his fingertips brush against my elbow. He was going to get me. I had tried my best and failed.

Suddenly, a glimmer of hope; a main street. Just before the guard's arms managed to encircle my waist, I turned left, heading out into the crowded street and away from the alley. As I reached the road, I started to scream.

'Help, help, SOS, he's trying to hurt me. Help, he wants to kill me!'

As I yelled, several people jumped, startled. The pedestrians glanced at me before their eyes slid to the guard chasing me. I could see the realization dawning on their faces. That was all the confirmation I needed. Turning, I fled before anyone could give me a second glance, not bothering to find out what would happen.

I just ran. I ran until I couldn't breathe, and then I ran some more. I kept making sharp turns and doubling back so it would be impossible to follow me. I kept running until finally I had to stop and throw up my guts. That's how she found me, curled up in a ball behind a bin, in an alley, puking.

'Sweet jesus, on a purple dragon, what happened to you?'

I turned and looking up I saw a girl, staring at me, her face a mixture of astonishment, amusement and confusion. She looked around sixteen or seventeen, the same age as me. She was tall with short, spiky hair that was a shocking shade of blue. Her face was pointed like an elf's and her large, brown eyes peered down at me, curiously.

'I'm Cassiopeia, I know me Ma must have been high as fuck when she named me, just call me Cassie,' she announced, grabbing my hand

and hauling me to my feet.

'Alice,' I mumbled, dragging my fingers through my long red curls, in an attempt to make myself more presentable.

'Well Alice, it's nice to meet you ... what happened? You escape from a mental institution or something?' She asked

'What, no of course not! Why would you think that?'

Instead of replying she simply dragged her eyes from my face down my body and then gave me a skeptical look, raising her eyebrows. Looking down at myself, I could kind of see where she was coming from. I was dressed in nothing but a hospital gown, my feet were bare and I was sure my hair was a complete mess. I was covered in sweat and grime and a little puke.

'Whatever, I don't judge. We get all sorts around here. How's about you come up to my flat with me and I can get you warmed up. You're probably hungry, right?'

I watched her warily as she turned but after standing still for a second, I decided to trust her and followed.

The flat was small and shabby but it was warm and I was in no position to complain. I followed Cassie into the bathroom, where she turned on the shower and handed me a towel that looked like it had been through the wash one too many times. Then she left me alone to wash off the grime.

When I finished, I pulled on some of the clothes that Cassie had left me. The jeans were a little long, but once I rolled them up they were fine. I headed back to the kitchen where Cassie handed me a plate of hot food.

We didn't talk much, both of us too invested in the meal, which we finished in seconds. I was exhausted by then and Cassie could see this so instead of pressing for the answers I knew she desperately wanted, she led me to the couch and handed me a pillow and a blanket before turning out the lights and leaving quietly. I was asleep the moment my head hit the pillow, not giving any thought to the events of the past few days.

16th November 2093

I woke up gasping for air, drowning under the sheets. Where was I? Glancing around the murky room, I was at a loss. Suddenly it all came back to me and I could barely move under the weight of it. Swallowing the sadness, I shoved the blankets off and stood, heading towards the kitchen.

When I entered, I found Cassie in her pajamas sitting on the counter, long fingers wrapped around a steaming mug of coffee. 'Morning' she chirped, hopping nimbly down from the counter and passing me the coffee, before turning back to pour herself another cup.

'I hope I didn't wake you, you looked so peaceful.'

'No' I mumbled, between sips of coffee. 'What time is it anyway?'

'Almost one, you slept for a while, you must have been really tired.'

'Uh huh. So, this is a nice place you have here, do you live alone?'

'Oh no, me Ma and I live here.'

'Where is she? I hope she doesn't mind me being here?' I asked, curiously.

'Out. She won't be home for hours so don't worry about it.'

We chatted idly for another few minutes, tiptoeing around the elephant in the room until Cassie couldn't handle it anymore.

'Okay, what's happened to you? I don't want to be nosy but seriously, you show up, confused, disorientated, completely manky, yet I gave you a place to stay and hot food. I think I deserve some answers.'

I thought about refusing to speak or fabricating some sort of lie, but looking into that girl's eyes, I couldn't help myself. As selfish as it may have been, I couldn't keep it to myself anymore and so, I told her everything.

***

'Let me get this straight. You are Alice Byrne, only child of Alistair Byrne, Minister of Covert Affairs, possibly the most hated man on this earth right now. And you think he's done something to your mother because she had something to do with the terrorist organisation *Foedus ad libertatem.*'

'Basically.' I nodded in agreement.

'You're crazy! I was right. You did escape from a mental institution.'

'I am not! It's true, all of it. What good would it do me to lie? I mean...' I trailed off when I noticed a small TV in a corner of the room, tuned to one of those 24-hour news stations.

Cassie noticed my distraction and turned around, following my eyes. 'What are you staring at?' But she trailed off too when she saw it.

On the screen was a large picture of me and my father – smiling at the photographer, arms linked. The photograph was captioned with the words 'Minister of Covert Affairs daughter kidnapped'. The screen switched back to a solemn anchor man, who cleared his throat before saying, 'The daughter of this nation's Minister of Covert Affairs, Alice Byrne, was kidnapped yesterday morning. She was spotted in Dublin city at around 2:30 yesterday afternoon, in a hospital gown, being chased by one of the assumed assailants. The federation strongly believe that she is still in the city, being held by the terrorist organization, *Foedus ad libertatem.*'

I gasped upon hearing the name of the organisation who might have all the answers. Hearing their name like that, on such a public platform strengthened my resolve to find them.

'Okay, I believe you,' Cassie interrupted my thoughts. 'I'm sorry I didn't believe you earlier but, well, it sounded crazy. Now I know and I promise I'll help you.'

'Help me?' I asked. 'You've only just met me.'

'But I can tell you need help. We all need help sometimes. Just tell me what you need.'

I stared at the girl – a girl I'd only met yesterday, who despite everything, was accepting me. Accepting me and willingly offering to help. Not many people I've known my entire life would do that for me, and yet, a teenage girl, no older than myself, would. I blinked slowly, not sure what to say. Instead I reached out my hand and clasped hers, my blue eyes locked on her large brown ones. 'Thank you Cassie, I don't...I can't....'

Instead of replying, she squeezed my hand, returning my smile. 'Just tell me what we need to do.'

'We need to find *Foedus ad libertatem.*'

After that we wasted no time. As Cassie rushed around the small flat shoving seemingly random objects into her tattered backpack, I asked about her mother and whether she might notice her daughter's sudden dissaperence.

'Oh don't worry about here she's hardly ever home and when she is she's usually too drunk to notice me.' She said this in an offhand manner as if it didn't really bother her but I could tell from the way her jaw stiffened and her fists clenched around the bag that it did.

'But just in case she does come home in a relatively sober fashion I left this for her,' Cassie announced waving a note under my nose. I just shrugged, not sure what I could say to this new information.

Soon – sooner than I had anticipated – we were out the door and down onto the street below, Cassie leading the way, twisting and turning through the alleys and smaller less crowded streets. I kept the hoodie Cassie had lent me zipped up tight, the hood pulled low over my face to prevent the few people we did encounter from recognizing me.

After almost an hour of this strange detour threw the city I had to stop Cassie. 'I don't want to sound like a bitch. I mean, I'm glad you agreed to help but I need you to tell me where we're going. We need to find the *Foedus ad libertatem* or somewhere we can get info on them.'

'Don't worry Alice, I'm not leading you on a wild goose chase around the city, I do have a destination in mind. As you're probably aware *Foedus ad libertatem* is quite a notorious organisation especially down here in the slums and poorer regions of the city.'

I shook my head in disbelief as this new information registered in my brain, I had never even considered the fact that people may not be happy with how the government was run. That they may even look to terrorism and violence as an appropriate means of protest. Cassie didn't mention my obvious ignorance and continued to speak.

'Anyway there's loads of graffiti around these parts that glorify them but the federation usually manage to clear it up pretty quick. Not much of the art gets left for more than a day or two, however there is one piece...'

'Tell me!' I gasped.

'There's an abandoned warehouse, one of those huge ones left over from the third world war. Anyway its completely covered in graffiti all dedicated to *Foedus ad libertatem*. The fed's used to be demented trying to get rid of it but as soon as they took part of it down, it would appear again the next day and they could never catch the culprits. Eventually they just fenced it off and left it. I figured that might be a good place to start.'

'Cassie you're a genius!' I gasped rushing forward to hug her. 'Quick take me to see this graffiti!'

'Calm down,' she laughed trying to squirm out of my tight embrace 'If memory serves it should be just around the corner.'

I quickly released her and allowed her to grab my hand, guiding me to the graffiti. It didn't take long, less than two minutes before we arrived outside a large abandoned warehouse, the entiore wall of one side completely covered in beautiful paintings and messages, the bright colors were a stark contrast to the dull and drab city which surrounded it. It was like a small oasis in a vast desert.

'Look there,' Cassie panted leading me threw a small gap in the fence and closer to the wall. I saw it, right where her finger was pointing *Foedus ad libertatem* was written in bold letters in the center of the artwork.

'MOTHER OF ALL THAT'S MYSTICAL, I KNOW WHAT THAT MEANS!!!' Cassie screamed in my ear.

'Wait what? How do you know what that means? Why didn't you say something?'

'Well I didn't know I knew until I saw it but now I know, you know?'

'TELL ME!!' I yelled unable to contain myself.

'It's Latin.'

'Latin? What's that?'

'It's an ancient language. Before the war there used to be hundreds of different languages, although even before the government made English the universal language Latin was pretty much dead.'

'How do you know it then, the teaching of any language which is not English is strictly forbidden in this day and age.'

'My Dad.' She sighed her eyes suddenly gained a faraway look to them 'He was a history lecturer in the city university. He found it in an old book and taught it to himself. He was teaching me but he never got to finish -the federation took him.'

I suddenly felt very ashamed to be the daughter of the minister for covert affairs. What was so bad about learning a new language? Did it really warrant being taken by the fed's? Everyone knew that once they took you, you were as good as dead. I could offer no words of comfort to Cassie so instead I squeezed her hand and gave her a reassuring smile. She returned it with a watery smile of her own.

Taking a deep shuddering breath she continued 'Anyway as I was saying I do know a little Latin and as far as I can tell this means league to freedom.'

A slow clap from behind us. I jumped, gripping Cassie for dear life. Spinning around we saw a tall man with greacy grey hair that fell into his dark hooded eyes emerging from the shadows. 'Well done you finally made it, about time too, we thought you'd never show.' His voice was low and smooth, like velvet. It didn't match his shaggy appearance. 'You must be Alice.'

'You already seem to know my name so I think its only fair that you tell me who you are,' I said sounding braver than I actually felt.

'Who I am is of very little concern to you, all you need to know is that I represent the organisation that you have been searching for.'

'*Foedus ad libertatem*?' I gasped.

'Correct.' the tall man acknowledged.

'But how did you know where to find me, why were you waiting here?'

'Why Cassiopeia told me of course! Now come along it's time to go.'

'Wait, no! Cassie I thought we were friend, why would you keep this from me?' I cried backing away from the two individuals.

'We are friends but I needed you to trust me. Everything I've told you about myself is true. I never lied, I simply withheld the truth. There's a difference.' She reached her hand out towards me. 'Come on, Alice, its time to take a stand. You need to trust us.'

I was still unsure about everything and I had no idea what my future held anymore, but taking a deep breath I bridged the gap between us grasping her hand and allowing her to lead me away with the shadow man, towards the unknown.

Brothers Betrayed
Eoghan McGleenan

A ship silently floats through space. The metal interior echoes the sound of the snoring crew and passengers. The captain lies awake; a feeling of unease grips him. He decides to take a walk around to try and calm his nerves. He never liked flying through this sector. Over the years it had been nicknamed the Bermuda in the centuries that people had flown through it. Ships had gone missing, vanishing without a trace. Not many, but enough to make people feel uneasy when flying through. The Captain sits at the helm of the ship and checks scanners, does a few routine checks and then looks out the window. Within seconds the alarm is sounded. The sleep-depraved crew jump up and run to their stations. The ship starts shaking from an impact. The Captain stares out, confused at why the scanners hadn't picked up anything. An enormous ship blocks his view. The ship continues to fire.

"Captain", the pilot who has just arrived shouts," shields have failed, engines are offline and our life support is about to go".

The Captain stares dumbstruck, unsure if it is just a dream. Screams echo around every corner of the ship as the enemy boards. Inexperienced and unsure of what to do the Captain waits. The doors burst open. The Captain hits the floor with a thud along with his crew. No one in the room is left alive.

***

Several soldiers walk through the lifeless ship. "Commander, two small life signs remain."

"Well go find them."

The soldiers enter the room to find two babies crying.

"Commander, two infants." He flicks through records on a nearby computer. "They appear to be twins, Commander." The Commander walks in.

"You know our orders, take one and kill the other."

The Commander hands one of the babies to a soldier and tells him to take him back to the ship. The soldiers leave with only the Commander staring at the baby. He takes out his pistol, decides against it and leaves the baby in his crib. Crying echoes throughout the ship as the attackers slip away into the unknown void.

***

"Preliminal scans suggest that the only living thing on board is an infant. Records suggest that it is one of two twins. They were the only children aboard."

Their ship slowly moves in and docks.

"What are we going to do with the kid?"

"You know our job, report our findings and destroy any evidence leftover."

"Woah, we are not killing a baby".

"Fine. Give it to the Captain; I'm pretty sure he mentioned that he knows a place for the baby to disappear."

"Now when you say disappear..."

"I don't mean kill him."

"Okay, okay. Come on let's take him back."

The wreck of the ship is vaporised as the Captain cradles the baby.

"A twin," he mutters to himself. "Still, my superiors are not going to be happy when they see this data."

***

The child was sent away to a secret facility on an officially uncharted planet. He was the perfect age for their training, their life and their changes. They had been kept hidden for centuries, almost millennia, by the galactic government. The child was changed, made to be better than any normal human. If the public knew of their existence, there would have been uproar, even though they protected the galaxy when they were needed. They would have claimed that every child that had gone there had lost their childhood and in many ways their humanity. In response they would have argued that the price paid for peace and the power he had been given was never too high. The process was long and monotonous. Every day he spent time in a lab being altered, improved. He was trained to fight, to be the best and to preserve the peace that had existed in the galaxy for centuries. At adulthood his robotic implants were installed. His body became a conduit of power fuelled by his DNA and his core. He could transfer his power to the weapons he used, creating pure, destructive energy. Their weapons were more powerful than any contemporary weapon. Those who were strong enough could increase their weapons' capabilities and could cause devastating effects, but few could sustain it for long. He lost twenty years of his life in a lab, but now he had centuries to make it back, his life span had been lengthened considerably. He always suspected something was different about him. His alterations stronger, he was more powerful. They told him his body and mind could take more than the others, but he was never told why.

His twin had a similar, yet more violent fate. His training was more intense. He had to be the strongest or he would have been eliminated by those who trained with him. Trained to use his emotions to keep him fighting, to make him more vicious. Those who threatened him, he was encouraged to kill. That way only the strongest would survive. As he made his way to adulthood, the pile of bodies left behind him increased as did his fury. When he finally reached adulthood he, like his brother, reached his full potential through robotic implants. He was the strongest, the fastest and the most ferocious of those who survived. Fighting the toughest challenges he could find and overcoming every one, he was trained to hate his enemy and show no mercy.

While one brother was trained to protect the galaxy, the other was trained to one day destroy it. When their training was complete they were almost unrecognisable as twins. One brother, Blaze, shaved his head; his skin had developed a pale complexion due to the years spent training in space with no real sunlight. Red markings and a long scar adorned his face and represented his fury and conquests. The other, Arius, kept his brown hair and retained a healthy look throughout his years of training. He never felt the need to change his appearance. Both were larger than any normal man, yet even for their size had incredible strength. A mixture of genetic and robotic modifications made them more intelligent, quicker to react and almost undefeatable in battle. Their only challenges could come from their own kind and incredible beasts across the galaxy. No ordinary human could challenge them.

***

"You have improved more than any of your opponents, why is that?" "I want it more, I push myself further, I am willing to do anything that is necessary," he replies in a deep voice.

"That is good. Remember it. I have placed you under my personal command. You should be honoured. No one has ever had the chance. No one has ever been strong enough. You are Blaze, born from fire and destruction." He smiles to himself.

"I will not disappoint General, we will succeed."

"It is time for us to strike, centuries of work will finally pay off soon because of you. I believe you will be key in this war. You will send a message to our enemies. Let them know that we have returned from exile."

***

"Our target is a secret intelligence base. Quick and easy, no mistakes. Follow my orders or I will kill you on sight. Stay out of my way and do your jobs".

The shuttle starts to shake as they enter the planet's atmosphere.

"We are now through their energy shield. Prepare for resistance, remember your training and strike fear in the hearts of our enemies." The shuttle stops moving and the doors open.

"Drop your weapons and surrender immediately, this is an unauthorised landing"

He laughs and replies viciously," Time to have some fun."

They charge. Sounds of shooting everywhere, but only one side are taking casualties. Hovering automatic turrets and small tanks start to surround them, but Blaze merely laughs as they try to do damage. Even though this is a secret base, the galaxy is peaceful and their weaponry is nothing compared to that of a group who have spent centuries planning for war. He races around the landing pad shooting any and all people in his path. A soldier tries to block him. He grabs him by the throat and flings his body away, his windpipe now crushed. They continue on through their enemies. He leaves his squad behind as a distraction and takes out his knife. He charges it up, slips inside before the blast shields close and continues unseen by the soldiers defending the base. Bodies hit the floor, unaware of what has happened to them as they die. Eventually, Blaze reaches a door.

"Locked," he murmurs to himself. He starts walking away, then runs at the doors. The doors explode killing anyone within a close radius. A group of ten soldiers remain blocking his path. They start firing. He dives and rolls while shooting back, his weapon far superior to theirs. Several thuds hit the floor, as he brushes himself off and laughs.

"Pathetic."

He starts hacking a console.

"Ready to send data now," he informs his pilot.

A minute later a ring tells him that it is complete. An explosion goes off at the side of the room. His squad finally catch up.

"Plant the bomb. We're done here. Blaze out"

***

Light-years away, a man stares at his brother on a monitor unaware of who he is. Their base on high alert. A man stands in front of a monitor.

"A day ago one of our intelligence bases was attacked by an unknown group. This is the footage we have. They stole data, some of which contains information about us. The damage this group could cause and what they intend to do next is unknown, but we're preparing for the worst. It is likely that this group now knows our location and will attack again soon. We have all spent decades training, some have spent centuries, but it is now time to put your training to use. Every one of you is being deployed to key locations. Next time they attack, we will be ready. Our job is to protect those at risk. Be ready. We have remained hidden in the dark up till now. That may change".

Arius finishes staring at his brother and asks," Who are these guys and why are they modified. I thought they were banned and only we had the facilities for it to take place".

The man at the monitor replies," We cannot confirm this groups identity, but will inform you when the time is right. Dismissed."

***

A man walks into the General's chambers. "Sir, the attack was a success and we have begun to separate the information that we have obtained."

The General smiles.

The officer continues, "There is however a complication, your new protégé, his twin who was reported as dead is alive and has undergone similar modifications to his brother. The data we found suggests that he was the only survivor on a ship that we destroyed. It seems that whoever was in charge of the mission didn't have the stomach to kill a child. He has been trained by our enemies and named Arius. He now stands in our way of domination."

"You are dismissed. Have the officer that reported him dead executed and tell Blaze to prepare for his next mission."

The General stares outside his window into the void.

"This could make him more powerful than I originally thought ... perhaps too powerful."

***

A shuttle flies through the atmosphere of a planet, heading towards the seat of government of the galaxy. It hovers in the courtyard of a huge building. A man jumps out and hits the ground with a thud. Dusting himself off, he walks towards the entrance. As he opens the door he is kicked backwards. Blaze looks at his attacker and smiles.

"Finally a challenge."

They both charge at each other and start firing. As they get close they knock each other's guns away. They start fighting hand-to-hand using countless numbers of fighting skills and techniques. Punching, kicking, blocking. Their attacks cause sparks and crackling in each other's shields.

Eventually Blaze pulls out his knife, charges it and roars angrily, "Prepare to die."

Arius laughs and takes out his own dagger. He starts to look strained as he charges it up. His dagger extends, now more of a sword. They continue fighting, but Blaze is unable to get close enough to do any damage, further increasing his rage. He shouts, charging his own dagger till it extends. The sheer power required to do this strains the two men as they grimace in pain. His weapon is now filled with his fury and more powerful than before. As their weapons clash, a huge explosion occurs. The courtyard lies in ruins, the two enemies now lie on the ground injured. The shuttle returns and lands, it picks up its limping cargo and leaves as a crowd gathers underneath the shadow of the huge building, which now has a gaping hole behind them. Soldiers and armoured vehicles now line the streets.

***

"Sir, another success. As you predicted the fight between the two brothers caused a devastating reaction. Their DNA and genetic makeup mixed with their modifications reacted violently. Our examinations show that it has increased his modifications' and his body's effectiveness and made him more powerful. Some of his cells appear to have mutated further than any of our own work could have done. If I could figure out how this happened I might be able to recreate and amplify the effects."

"There is no need, I already know enough. Dismissed." The General licks his lips and smiles maniacally. "Time for panic".

***

After the fight, Arius was brought before his elders for questioning. The Archon, the head elder, asks him worriedly," And you are sure that is exactly what happened?"

"Yes, I'm sure. Now what happened? Why was there an explosion?"

"I'm not sure how it is possible but…."

Crackling from a nearby monitor distracts them and a man appears on the screen and begins to talk.

"The recent destruction of your precious government's building was no accident. It was caused by fighting. The peace is over. Most of you will have forgotten about us, but we have returned from our exile."

The screen flickers and a video of the battle in the courtyard shows. A flash of light appears from the explosion and the man reappears.

"It is time for you worms to panic, we are better than you, more advanced and we will crush you. Your government has harboured some of our kind for centuries, hidden in the shadows, carrying out tasks that no normal person could achieve. The fighting I have shown you is only the beginning. Those who were harboured by your government should have been executed as your pathetic galactic law states. Prepare for war, you will be caught in the middle of it."

As the screen fades everyone stands stunned.

"He's alive," the Archon mutters. After a few moments of silence the room explodes with shouting and unanswered questions

Outside the hall everyone has finally filtered off. The Archon talks in private with Arius.

"Very little of our history has been made known to even some of our oldest members. Centuries ago we were a ruling faction in a newly inhabited galaxy, but our group split over differences. Some of us wanted to control the weak and make them work for us and for a time that is how it was. However a group of us grew tired of the tyranny. We wanted a peaceful galaxy, where the ordinary would be considered equal and would have power too. It caused all-out war. Brother fought brother, sister fought sister and friends killed each other because of the sides they chose. At the end of the war both our groups were decimated, few remained. From the rubble, ordinary people set up their own government. We agreed to help them and exiled those who had once fought with us. Officially we were all exiled and our modifications became outlawed. For centuries we have helped the government create peace. The man you just saw, he was once my friend and became my enemy. Towards the end of the war he led our enemies and took the title the General. I thought he was dead."

"Why are you telling me this now, Why not before?" Arius responds angrily.

"It was part of our deal. In order to train new members, we promised to keep them in the dark about our own past."

"So you're telling me that the only reason we're allowed to exist is because the government needs us, even after all we sacrificed." He turns to leave but then doubles back.

"What happened down there, the explosion I mean," he asks curiously.

The Archon replies, "We have seen similar reactions before between twins."

"None of us have family, you know that."

"At first we thought the power of twins was a great asset, but time and time again, they became jealous of one another and caused immense destruction, often killing each other in the process. You had a twin, but he was reported dead when you were found." He pauses.

"The more you fight him the more powerful you will become, but also more dangerous. Sometimes the reaction can destroy both twins in the process. This is a lot to take in, so I'm going to let you think about it yourself."

As the Archon left, Arius stood there jaw slightly agape, trying to comprehend what he had just been told. A galaxy away Blaze was told the same truth as Arius and stood confused about his brother. It was the first time he had ever doubted himself and more importantly the General.

***

Sitting in his bed, he stares at a corner of the ceiling. With a furrowed brow, he tries to mull over what the Archon has just told him, while keeping one eye on a nearby screen. The screen shows panic every-where. Protests about what the public had just discovered. People are afraid that what they saw was only just a taste of what is to come. Anger. Anger at the government for hiding them for centuries. Anger at those who now threaten them, and fear. He tries to ignore it all, but his strained face shows that he is thinking about the implications of what he has just learned and what is to come.

***

A man walks through an office in a suit, clearly not meant to house his physique. He gets odd glances as he walks by, but people are too busy and too panicked to bother to react.

"Pathetic," he thinks to himself.

Finally he arrives at a huge door with several guards. Two walk up to him.

"Do you have an appointment?"

"No," he replies bluntly, clearly bored of the situation.

"Then please vacate the area."

"Oh, but they'll want to see me".

He grabs the two guards and throws them at the others, ripping his suit in the process. Dazed, the guards lie on the ground, unsure at what has happened. Before they react the man forces the door open and walks inside a brightly lit room.

"What is the meaning of this? How did you get past our scanners?!"

Laughing he replies," I don't need a weapon to kill you, I am a weapon. I am Blaze.

An alarm goes off, the only sign that a government that had stood on the foundations of the people for centuries is about to fall.

***

An alarm on a monitor starts blaring. "Emergency SOS, government in danger, help needed. Will I divert course to new location?"

"You get me there as fast as possible."

Arius sits back down in his shuttle aware that his brother is attacking and why. As the shuttle touches down, he hits the ground running. Swarms of guards converge on the entrance. As he walks in he notices the bodies littering the floor, several of his own kind lie savagely beaten and lifeless. An example made to discourage anyone from following the assailant. He gives chase through the halls and finally catches up on the roof.

Sweat drips from his brow as he shouts, "Coward."

Blaze turns around.

"So my 'brother' has finally come back to me," he exclaims sarcastically, straining the word brother.

"You're no brother of mine, look at what you did to those people."

"It was all in good fun, 'brother'. Enough talk, now you die," he shouts as he begins to attack.

He furiously starts beating his brother, who has become off-balance.

Eventually Arius' shield explodes, forcing Blaze back. As he falls back he is attacked and a knife swings for his neck, but his enemy is tired and he knocks it out of his hand. "You're finished 'brother', even without a weapon I can easily defeat you."

He continues to attack, smashing Arius further into the roof. Small explosions occur with every hit, affecting neither of them. Bone breaks as Blaze continues. A shout from the door distracts him. Several people stand at the door, all modified. They open fire, sending pure energy towards their target. He jumps off the building as the firing continues. Seconds later a shuttle flies up with Blaze in the doors, looking angrily at the people firing at him. He had lost his prey. The shuttle silently flies away, its mission now complete.

***

Arius lies there watching shots blasting behind him and his brother escaping. He tries to get up, but darkness clouds his vision and he blacks out. A dreamless sleep envelops him.

When he finally awakes he finds himself in a sterile white room, surrounded by machinery. He tries to sit up, but a sharp pain in his head prevents him, as he grimaces. A message appears on a nearby screen and a voice echoes through the room. "Patient is now awake."

A few seconds later the Archon walks in and asks calmly," How are you feeling?"

"Terrible, how long was I out?"

"Considering what you have been through you're lucky to be alive. The attack was three days ago and considering the circumstances, your healing has been remarkable. No doubt due to the effects of fighting with your brother."

"What happened?"

The Archon hesitates and then replies," The galaxy is in disarray, the government is no more and the galaxy has no leadership. We've tried to communicate with people, but they threaten us and blame us. There are next to no defences on most planets, but that's not the worst part. Reports of an invasion have been given to me, planet communications go dark and with no defence, I fear for the worst."

"They shouldn't be able to take planets that easily; surely they've used their shield generators to prevent any attack from space."

"The government on each planet controls their defences and in many cases have been overthrown by rioters, making it easy for the invasion to proceed. Those planets that do have shields merely slow down the invasion and eventually fall by a ground assault. We still have our own defences, but they won't do much against a ground assault. If the pattern continues they'll be here within a matter of days."

***

"General, I have completed our goals, the government has fallen and our invasion should be easy."

The General replies," You have done well Blaze, however, your brother still lives and, therefore he is still a threat. A threat which must be crushed. We will deal with him later, our enemies have retreated to their own planet and are readying themselves. "Prepare yourself for a ground assault"

"As you wish General, my brother is weak, do not worry about him." He turns to leave but then stops to report," I can feel my strength growing, the reaction was stronger this time, but it affected me less.

The leader replies, smiling evilly, "Good, then it looks unlikely that the reaction will kill you."

"You never told me that the reaction could kill me."

"That does not matter now. Focus your strength, your rage and your power."

"Will I be leading the assault?"

"No, we will need all of our strength to eliminate this threat. This is personal, I must lead the assault, but before that I want you to hunt down any spies we discover on any planets.

He salutes the General and barks," I itch at the chance to eliminate our only threat. I need a proper challenge." He walks away, to ready himself.

The General sits down and mutters to himself, "Perhaps not our only threat."

***

Finally out of his hospital bed, Arius begins to train, angry at what has happened. After an hour he goes to talk to the Archon and the other elders. He barges in to their meeting area covered in sweat.

"Why are we waiting, we should be taking the fight to them."

The Archon hushes the other elders and replies calmly," If we attack them head on they will annihilate us. Their ships' weaponry is more advanced, they've had centuries to improve and make incredibly powerful weaponry. Everything we have done has been in secret, many of our strongest weapons are used for stealth."

He grunts angrily and replies, "We should be doing something."

"You must calm yourself; your anger will make you open to mistakes when you fight. One of our spies managed to send me a message about the invasion, but was being hunted by your brother. Our only chance to beat them is to conserve our forces and wait for them. Their forces will be spread thin and for every soldier they lose, it will make our jobs easier."

"So we let them slaughter millions, maybe billions while we wait. Our job is to protect them, even if they don't appreciate it."

"If we attack now, we'll get ourselves killed and who can we help then." Angrily Arius walks away knowing that what he has been told makes sense.

"Doesn't mean I have to like it," he mutters angrily.

***

An alarm sounds noisily. Everybody is aware of what is happening, but

115

no one wants to believe, believe that this could be their end and the galaxy's. Time seems to pass in slow motion as people prepare, getting equipment and weapons. Years of training all come down to this battle.

"Ship sighted, identification unknown, large transport class, no visible weaponry, but strong shields are active. Virus detected in sys…." A familiar voice sounds.

"Your government exiled us, but they also exiled you. They only accepted you to use you, but now reject and hate you, even though you fight for them. Our groups used to be one, we had a brotherhood, and we called each other brother and sister. I want it to be the same way. When we were on the brink of galactic domination, your leaders betrayed us, they betrayed you and gave power to the weak. But we are all stronger than the worms that have been crushed to get here. We will land momentarily. Throw down your arms, join us and be worshipped as Gods or face annihilation and join the worms in the dirt beneath our feet. The choice is yours."

An army stands outside the last stronghold in the galaxy. They watch the ship as it comes closer, aware of the offer that has been made. The anti-air defences are offline. After starting to fire on the ship, they were almost immediately hacked and became useless. Air is forced out of the way as the ship lands. The ship doors open and an army begins to march, with two figures leading them. They stop halfway between both armies and wait. On the other side of what will soon become a battleground, the Archon orders Arius, his new protégé, to join him as he walks to meet them. He looks at his brother. At first he thought they looked nothing alike but now he sees similarities. His facial structure, beneath his hate filled eyes he can see a hint of blue and they are built similarly.

"I thought you were dead," the Archon comments bluntly.

"Death will not stop my vengeance, traitor. I used to call you an ally, but today you will fall," he bellows angrily.

A cheer from his army sounds as he finishes.

"I have made my offer, now who will take it."

Several people glance at each other and a few amble over, fear visible in their eyes. An angry stare from Arius greets them as they cross the halfway mark.

Blaze laughs and comments," You look angry Arius, well let's see how you look when you and the Archon lie dead beneath my feet. I am Blaze and you will be consumed in the flames of my rage." Arius grunts in reply and walks away.

Both armies wait, a sudden calmness descends over them. Then all hell breaks loose. Both armies charge, the sounds of pure energy being fired in all directions. As they charge, the Archon is separated from Arius. He starts firing, cutting down those in his path, taking out his knife when they get too close, all the time looking for the Archon and his true enemy. Then he sees them. Two leaders now fight. People around them trying to stay out of their way, they battle fiercely. Dodging, shooting, firing.

"You have grown weaker since we last fought Archon," the general laughs mockingly.

The fighting continues. They finally get close enough and try to fire at each other, but push each other's weapons away as they fire. They try to fire again, but the General gets angry and smashes his opponent's gun. In response the Archon pulls out his knife, swings and knocks the General's weapon away. They stand back a few paces.

"It is time for you to see my new masterpiece."

The General pulls out a hilt from his belt and charges it.

"With this I can create any weapon I want, no more knives and no more wasting huge amounts of energy to extend it."

He charges it and creates a sword. He strikes furiously sensing victory. The Archon blocks what he can with his knife but mid-swing the General's weapon changes to a scythe and strikes the Archon. He collapses to the ground.

"I have trained everyday waiting to repay you for your betrayal. Now your debt will be paid."

He strikes the Archon, finishing him off. A shout rings across the battlefield.

"No!" Arius starts charging, consumed by anger, ready to kill the General. As he gets close, he is knocked down by his brother, who then shoots him. He crashes to the ground as he hears his brother laugh.

"Kill him now, prove that you are the stronger brother."

Blaze blocks his brother's path to the General, so he focuses his attention on his brother. He lashes out furiously, trying to slice his brother's neck open. He misses and becomes off- balanced. Trying to strike again, he is knocked over by his brother. A soldier wanders too close and is immediately killed. Lying on the ground, his brother once again devastates him with multiple hits. He leaves him lying in the dirt and returns to the General's side.

"All of the threats to us have been eliminated."

"Not all of them," he replies, as he swings his weapon again.

Both brothers lie down in the dirt, one struck down by the other and the other stabbed in the back by the General.

"You have proven to me that you are too powerful to be kept alive, there is no other way for me to assert full control. Goodbye."

He stares into his eyes. Raises his scythe up. Finally he brings it down. Before it can connect the General is kicked across the battlefield. Lying on the ground, Blaze is helped up by his brother. They both stare at each other and understand each other for the first time. They have a common enemy now and together they could become unstoppable. They turn to face the General, one calm, one filled with fury, both ready to fight and die. The General screams loudly, runs at them and arcs his scythe. The three weapons collide, creating a blinding explosion.

When the dust settles only the two brothers remain standing, the rest either dead or unconscious. Trying to contain the unconscious General, Arius walks over, but is shoved by his temporary ally. With one strike the General is dead. Blaze spits on the dead body grabs the General's weapon and destroys it.

Blaze faces his brother and says bluntly, "He needed to die, the stupid old hypocrite. All his talk about being betrayed and then he tries the same on me."

"You shouldn't have killed him," Arius replies.

"He never even understood his own teachings. Our existence is based on making what is weak stronger, not making weapons that are easy to use," Blaze shouts angrily at no one in particular.

"What do we do now?" his brother asks.

"You can't defeat me so don't try. You're not worth my trouble. I'm taking what's left of my army and leaving. The General only wanted revenge. All I want is a challenge and galactic domination bores me. Spending the rest of my existence on a throne doesn't excite me."

"Why don't you join us?"

He laughs and replies," I don't think so. You're the good guys remember. You'll have to go and rebuild the galaxy. Don't try to change who I am. My goal is to become more powerful. We will leave you in peace for now, but one day I will return and then we will see who is truly better."

"What about your survivors?"

"If they're not strong enough to follow me, they can rot for all I care."

"The elders won't let you just leave."

"But you will because we're brothers and we're all that we've got. Don't chase after me or I will end you."

Arius thinks to himself and then replies calmly," No. You've caused enough damage to this galaxy. I'm not going to just let you leave, knowing that you are stronger than me and can come back again. This is between you and me."

Blaze replies angrily, "I gave you and this galaxy a chance but if you don't want it, fine."

They face each other and attack. A blur of fists, legs and weapons now decide the future of the galaxy. Both brothers fight ferociously, knowing what is at stake. Anger flows through one, but the other finally understands his teachings. He is calm and he is not going to lose this fight. It is his duty, to the galaxy and to his brother. Blaze's fist glances across his face, but he ignores it. He blocks everything that is thrown at him, not fighting out of anger but fighting for what he believes in. Sometimes to protect, you have to destroy. Blaze now strikes more viciously than before, with worry in his eyes. A wild strike misses its target and seconds later Blaze is on the ground, struck down by his brother.

"You have been defeated, accept it. You may be my brother, but I fight for more than myself. I can't lose because if I do I will have let down all the people I swore to protect. I can't lose because then you will be lost forever and I will have never had a true brother."

Blaze curses back at him, the excruciating pain from the knife in his stomach visible in his eyes, its power coursing through his body.

Blaze spits at him and replies, "Don't preach to me, I've already made my choice. You'll have to kill me or I will kill you."

"Too many people have died in this conflict."

"Then you're a fool. I will never stop, as long as I live everything you protect is at risk."

Arius turns away and replies, "Sometimes the risk is worth the re-ward … brother. We all make our own choices. So leave now and never return, if you do I will not hesitate to kill you. We're brothers and we're all that we've got. Don't forget it."

Blaze's ship silently touches down beside him. Defeated he crawls inside and turns to face the chaos. Bodies lie strewn across the battle-field. A crater dominates the centre, where the explosion emanates from. As the ship flies away, he catches a final glimpse of Arius' face.

Calm and collected, his brother stares back and as the ship flies away to return to where it came from. Arius sighs and hopes that he will never see him again.

***

The galaxy was in ruins, but for now there would be peace. Both the General and the Archon died in the battle, but from the rubble two brothers rose. Their experience changed them both. Neither could tell if their change was for better or for worse, but they both understood themselves, their power and they knew their change was necessary to lead. As the invasion ended and the invaders left under their new General, the new Archon tasked himself with rebuilding the galaxy and fixing the damage that had been done. Finally there was peace and for now there was no foreseeable reason for it to be broken.

Underwater Ruins
Sarah Moore

September 19th, 1940

Just six months after the rebellion and the once thriving city was already falling apart. It was revolutionary, it changed things forever. Having an underwater city was unique and depicted as "The end of overcrowding!" Luxury was the theme throughout the city. Extravagance and elegant lifestyles were how people lived here before. It was a fresh start for anyone. Some people arrived without a penny, some covered in riches, it didn't matter. When the project was finished , throngs of people fled to the submarines that were to be catapulted deep into the ocean. There were riots, people were willing to kill to get a place to this "New World".

A few months after we had all arrived, one man stood outside The Grand Hall where all politicians worked and where the city was run from. This man with booklets and posters stood on the steps of The Grand Hall for hours, proclaiming his feelings about the city, how he missed nature, the seasons, everything on the surface, how we were trapped here like rats for the rest of our lives, how it was inhuman. Soon, hundreds of people became involved, protesting that they wanted to leave, the answer was no. More than 80% of the politicians were extreme loyalists, they had great pride in the city and what would the city be without people? After refusing the people the choice of leaving, there was an uprising and the city fell apart, many politicians fled in escape pods, so many died and a few were left stranded like us.

***

I was tired of looking out the glass pane and seeing the ocean floor. I wanted to see the world, feel the wind on my face, and feel the glow of the sun as it glistened on my skin again. It was just me, Sarah, my little sister, Martha, and my dad Jack Moore. My mam had died only weeks before because of a lack in S-light.

I paced around my room and stared out the door to see my sister staring back at me with her little toothless smile ,which seemed like an attempt to make everyone a little happier. I looked back at the giant wall, water dripped down the glass and puddles of water lay on the floor. Soon, there would be nothing left of this place and water would submerge the entire city. We had been unsure, how damaged parts of the city actually were, so we tended not to go far. So you could imagine, travelling around for basic supplies was difficult.

The entire city was themed like a submarine, with huge, metal, round, bronze doors and the circular hatch, connecting each dome. Most doors were kept open as they were heavy and hard to re-open. I stumbled across the room to the door, avoiding any puddles of water. The murky ground was cold against my bare feet. My dad was already awake, searching the cupboards for whatever food was left in this apartment, we would be moving to a nearby place soon, once the food here was gone.

"Good morning, beautiful," Dad said, whilst kissing Martha's forehead.

You could tell by his appearance that inside he was dying. Not sick or terminally ill, but my mam had been everything to him. Martha and I had to listen to him sob most nights.

The top button on his shirt was unbuttoned and his tie was slung around his neck. Martha pulled up a chair and with a struggle she climbed up on it to sit down, her legs dangling over the edge. She yawned and playfully giggled as she messed with her golden blonde hair. I was the eldest, turned sixteen two weeks before the rebellion. He tried to avoid me, only because I was the image of my mam and seeing me only reminded him of Mam. We all sat around the small round table and nibbled on cold food. There was dead silence until my dad spoke.

"I think it's time we try moving from this area," he explained.

"But the flooding at the door to the Region? And the door is closed, it'll be hard to open," I stated.

"Not to be blunt but we will run out of food and there's no S-LIGHT left so soon enough we will die, Sarah."

"I'm being realistic."

I stood up and walked out to look across the balcony to see if it was actually possible to open the door. There were one hundred apartments in this district, we were the only people. The glass dome was leaking very badly near it and you could see some of the door was already blocked by water.

Later in the day, my dad came into the room where I was reading Martha a book that I had found, which was not sodden wet. He knocked on the door to interrupt and Martha ran over and jumped into his arms, he picked her up and spun her around, turning to look at me.

"I have thought about it and we need to open the door by getting rid of, or pushing aside, the water long enough to jam open the door," I explained to my dad.

"Yes I agree," he replied.

September 24th, 1940

The food was practically gone in this place and in most of the other apartments. Using buckets, bowls, cups and whatever we could find, we scooped as much water as we could, as quickly as we could, out of the doors way. Martha stood watch as me and my dad did the work. With sweat dripping off our faces and drips of water, dripping from the dome ceiling, we finally managed to shift the water, throwing it to the side. Opening the door would prove a more difficult challenge. The door had a small window above the hatch. It was high up so Martha grabbed on to my dad's leg and climbed his body like a tree, awkwardly, nearly falling many times. She clung to him closely. She stood up fully on his shoulders and spread her arms to reach a dent in the hatch. She then pulled herself up to stare through the window, which was slippery and she struggled to hold on. Her jaw dropped and she started breathing excitingly.

"What do you see?" I asked, intrigued.

"Others," she replied.

My dad and I stared at each other in shock and suddenly there was complete silence and all that could be heard was the drip, dripping of water to the cold, murky, metal floor.

My dad quickly grabbed Martha off his shoulders and put her on the ground and started trying to jam open the door frantically. He struggled and grunted as his hands kept slipping. He yelled in frustration and banged loudly on the metal with all his might, but it was no use, no one heard. He slid down, leaning against the door and sat on the wet ground, his head in his palms. I sat down beside him and patted his shoulder in comfort.

"We'll find a way," I whispered.

It was then I looked around to see what had become clear, our family had changed so much. Martha's face looked drained and flushed. And Dad, weak, his skin pale. And then I glanced down at myself, my clothes stained and damp. I had become so thin; my knees looked as though they would buckle at any moment. Staring at the ground, something golden caught my attention. I stood up and picked up a plank of metal off the ground revealing the beautiful thing. Engraved on the bottle was S-LIGHT.

"Drink it!" I said quickly and shoved it into my dad's hands.

"No you and Martha need it more," he replied.

S-LIGHT, what most people here had so badly longed for. Without sunlight people grew weaker and weaker and would eventually die, drinking S-LIGHT was like being given a shot of adrenaline straight through your heart. It was just what we needed now.

"If you have this you will definitely be able to open the door," I explained.

He picked up the golden bottle, which was glowing like it actually had sunlight trapped in it, wanting to burst out of the bottle to bounce and reflect off the walls. Even though we knew he needed it to open the door I glanced over at my sister. Her eyes were droopy, her skin losing colour. Even though we couldn't have it, what if we didn't find anymore? Would my sister die? After these thoughts in my head, my dad had begun drinking the bottle. He jumped up and threw the empty bottle to the ground, smashing it into tiny pieces. His eyes were glowing, he seemed so alive, he had so much energy. He locked his hands on the door and turned the handle like it was covered in butter. He slowly pulled it and stood back as it gradually swung open. Martha hid behind his leg. The silence was deafening.

We walked into the even bigger dome. This part of the city was used a market before the rebellion so hopefully there would be lots of food available. We walked a bit inwards and stopped to look around; strangely I could hear music, old jazz, the sort of nostalgic music you'd hear in a bar late at night. We were suddenly startled at the sound of a smashing plate. Maybe Martha had been right? Were there people here? How else could there have been the music or the sound of the shattering plate? We slowly looked around us and saw a shutter on a window creak open. A head popped out.

"ARE YOU ARMED?" the man shouted across at us.

Slowly but carefully we raised our arms and turned around to indicate we were not.

"WHO'S THAT BEHIND YOU LAD?" he shouted sternly.

My heart was beating rapidly, I felt relieved that we had made it this far but I didn't want to cause a dispute with whoever lived in this dome. Martha crept out from behind my father and only her small self could have defused the situation so well. She looked up at the man, whose face was harsh , stress lines dented far into his brow.

She just smiled brightly and said

"Can you help us?"

Suddenly, out came small groups of people from different buildings. We were amazed how many people there were. Even if it was only ten to fifteen people, we had been nearly certain that we were the only ones. The man who we had talked to pushed his way through the small crowd to talk to us.

"Welcome! Welcome!" the man eagerly said while gripping my dad's hand into a friendly and firm handshake.

"We were sure the District was empty!"

"Yes we were the only ones left, the door caused some trouble to open," Dad replied.

He directed us around, showing us what everything was. There were so many supplies, like food and S-LIGHT here. Martha and my father stared in awe but the entire time my mind was focused on the young boy whose stare I could feel directly on me.

The boy was about my age, most people would describe him as attractive but something else about him caught my attention. His eyes were sparkly blue, his skin pale and his hair chocolate brown. He was quite lanky, tall. He looked as though he was clumsy and awkward. A slight smile appeared on his face when he realised I too was staring at him. I felt heat in my cheeks and I was suddenly blushing. Then focusing on what everyone else was doing, I paced quickly over to my dad and sister.

Soon after, we were shown to a place where we could stay and we settled down to get some rest. It had been a busy day, we had learnt so much about here. There were scientists in the other building, working on fixing old escape pods to get back to the surface. There were just ordinary people carrying out the simple task of retrieving supplies for the scientists. And lastly, there were the people in charge, former solicitors and politicians, including the man we had met today. The people in charge, tried to arm themselves with whatever they could find against the other dome. There was so much we were unaware of, like that the dome behind was empty, nicknamed "No Man's Land", because the gates on both sides were easy enough to open but, on the other side of the other gate was not a place anyone here would dare to enter. While our small community was all set on getting to the surface to escape this dilapidated place, they wanted to restore the city to its former glory, and hence this is partially how the small feud began.

The other dome connected to "No Man's Land" was made up of the extreme loyalists who believed the city could still be restored and made great again and didn't want any other survivors leaving. Inside "No Man's Land" there were tunnels connecting to rooms and halls with supplies but since the other group did not want the scientists trying to get to the surface, whenever people from our group tried to retrieve supplies from these tunnels the others took drastic action. "No Man's Land" turned into a war zone.

So much to take in, in one day, had our family just entered a battle zone?

September 29th, 1940

We are settling in well here, things seem moderately okay and we have made new friends. I managed to talk to the young boy I had seen the first day we came here. I found out his name is Peter, quite tragically, both of his parents are within the 'bad' dome (as some people here call it). They were separated during the rebellion because of an argument that had started between them. Although he does agree with our group more so than the other. Soon enough, our people could leave this god forsaken place and breathe fresh air, feel wind brush past our legs, feel real sun glisten on our faces, but most importantly live again or for Martha, start living.

At the end of the day as I settled into bed, pulling the itchy blanket over me, I began to think about the other dome. Surely, they would start to realise that we are actually progressing and something big was about to happen. I just hope that thing turns out to be good.

October 3rd, 1940

Finally the day is soon approaching. Tomorrow we should hopefully, use the escape pods to reach the surface and navigate our way to land. From clever scientists to charismatic politicians, to ambitious citizens, we had all worked hard, as had everyone else to accomplish our survival. Tonight there shall be celebrations, a dance, a feast with whatever food remains, use up all the supplies left. Sure why not? We leave tomorrow, we'll have everything we need once we return to the surface.

Not much had occurred in the last few days. Last trips were made for supplies and I attempted to talk to Peter more. In the general sense I had a small feeling that he liked me but I didn't mind because I sort of liked him too. Sometimes when I talked to him he would slowly lean closer and closer towards me. And our conversations generally lasted hours, we had so much in common. He was even great talking to Martha, which made him that little bit more attractive. Yesterday we had an interesting conversation...

I was packing things quickly into metal cases, making sure they were tight together and tidy. I felt a slight tap on my back and startled, I turned around quickly. It was Peter.

"Good Afternoon," he said cheerily.

"How can you tell? All the clocks are broken," I replied, giggling flirtatiously.

"Ah well you see my grandfather gave me this pocket watch before we came down here, indestructible I'd say."

"Oh, very nice," I replied, bending over to see the so called indestructible watch.

"I was wondering... maybe... if you want.... you would consider attending the celebrations tomorrow avec moi?" he asked, a cheeky smile appearing on his face.

"And why would I consider going with you?" I replied also with a cheeky smile.

"It'll definitely be worth your while I assure you,"

"Well I have nothing to lose, I accept."

And with my response he flashed a big smile, clasped his hands together, turned on his heels and proudly walked off.

October 4th, 1940

I was looking forward to the celebrations. Inside me and my sister's bedroom, we chatted and laughed as I plaited her hair and then put her in clothes that were way too big. There was a sense of joy, enthusiasm, great happiness amongst everyone. I carefully placed my hair in a bun, tidying it with some pins, letting a few strands of hair let loose at the front. The curls bounced in front of my face.

And with that we headed outside together to join everyone. There was a gramophone out playing loudly and people toasting drinks with chipped glasses and from the corner of my eye I saw Peter leaning against a nearby stall, staring at me. He rushed over and gazed up and down at me.

"Beautiful," he whispered in my ear.

I cannot describe how much I blushed. He gently grabbed my hand and we ran over to dance. I followed quickly and looked back at my sister who was jumping up and down giggling.

The rest of the night I talked to nearly everyone but Peter never seemed to stay by my side, he seemed distracted and somehow anxious.

We listened to the scientists explain how they fixed the pods and we listened to stories of peoples' lives before the rebellion. It was the most fun I had had in years, even though I had only known these people a few days we all felt a feeling of togetherness. I had even seen my dad dancing with some woman, and I was happy for him, he saw me looking and smiled. I smiled back. After everything that had happened I really think our relationship had been made stronger.

October 5th, 1941

Everyone has decided to sleep out together and when I woke up I rubbed my eyes, looking at my surroundings. I then realised Peter was not here, maybe he had decided to go back to his room. I drifted back asleep shortly after.......

A few hours later I was awoken suddenly by my sister tickling me. Not the most pleasant way to wake up... but it was time to get up, everyone was on their feet bringing out bags and lifting crates. I was still wondering where Peter was and the people I asked said they had not seen him. Everything was calm as people did final jobs when suddenly one by one people from the other dome pushed their way through the door and there was a racket of shots fired upwards. We were under attack, I quickly looked around for Martha and my dad pushed her into me shouting,

"Go! I'll stay and try hold them off!"

And then I saw it, Peter, on their side, holding a rifle. For a few seconds it was as though time slowed as I shouted "Peter!" I shook my head in disbelief as he looked over and just simply smiled in the most evil way. My heart dropped and it felt as though someone had punched me in the stomach..

I clenched Martha's hand firmly and ran towards the escape pods. The scientists were trying to rush people into the pods

"GO! GO! GO!" they shouted.

I ran faster than I ever thought I could over cold ground, trying not to step on the dead and dying in my attempt to flee, still clinging to my sister's hand.

My father was fighting off one of the men and I whispered to Martha

"We can't leave him," Martha started sobbing, she was so scared, I could not even register how I felt at that moment.

And then I heard the three shots, the noise rang in my ear and echoed around the dome and my father fell, fell to the ground. It took four men from our group to stop us from running over and they picked us up and we were carried into the pod. The door was quickly closed and I was let free.

"Open this door right now!" I screamed.

"We can't, one of the pods they broke and there isn't room," a woman replied.

"I don't care! That's my father you can't just- you can't," and I burst into tears.

Quickly, the pod shot up through the tube and we were forced to watch the ones we had left behind fight and I just sat there not being able to look again at my father dead on the cold, wet ground. I wanted to keep him in my memory as the strong, loyal, loving and kind father he had been to both of us.

Hours later the water was becoming lighter, I lifted my head from my hands and glanced around slowly, mostly women and the odd child sat around. There were myself, Martha, five women, three men and another two children. Eight had been left behind. I wanted to feel lucky I really did, but in all honesty I felt one of the men left behind or my father deserved my seat so much more. How would I look after Martha? Would we be sent to an orphanage? Suddenly the pod creaked and one of the men (happening to be a scientist) explained to us we were close to the surface and then we all felt the pod floating in the water and sunlight flooded in across the pod. People shielded their eyes as for all of us it had been so long since we had experienced the feeling of the sun being too bright. I looked over at Martha, her face was pressed against the window, she had never seen the surface or the sun.

"So beautiful," she whispered.

"Don't stare directly at it," I muttered.

One by one we climbed out on top of the pod to look out and around. It was dawn, the sky was a mixture of mellow colours such as red and purple and orange. I felt the small heat on my face but the wind was overpowering. A loud terrifying machine like noise roared through the sky and we all looked up and stared at the fighter planes flying overhead. We watched in wonder but suddenly a large metal tin dropped from each the planes and we watched them drop on land far away. They were bombs. Explosions began all over. We stared in horror, what had we arrived into?

Life Beyond Pretty Flowers and Fairytales
Rachael Murray

My name is Charlie. I am a nine year old girl and I am a hunter. Not a hunter who kills animals. Or people. I am a hunter of supernatural beings. Some people may or may not believe in such things, but they are real. If you don't believe in them because you haven't seen anything, it's either because I'm doing my job well or because most supernatural things have human forms. Let's hope it's the first one.

You may not believe me because of my age but I'm not joking when I say I know what I'm doing. I've grown up with this stuff. My parents were hunters. Before the accident.

My mom is not the same since Father died. Mom used to be happy, she sort of gave up on hunting when I was born. I doubt she was upset about that though. She would only hunt when Father really needed her. Therefore, she was a stay at home mom for the most part. I loved coming home from school and smelling freshly baked Betty Crocker cookies. It always cheered me up after a hard day in school. The smell would instantly calm me down.

She's still strict though, maybe even more now. I obviously miss my dad but it's hard to talk about. Especially since he passed so recently.

My dad died very tragically. When he came across a leviathan nest, the fight was too much for him. It was horrific to see the aftermath. My mother couldn't handle herself and completely broke down at the funeral. There wasn't even anything to bury. It was more just a mass. Tears were shed. Fellow hunters came along. That is how I got involved.

I spoke to some of the well-known hunters and began to figure out the jist of things. Many people told me how important the work my dad did was and how he died on very good terms. Therefore after the teary eyed funeral, I was inspired.

***

'I'm going out, Mom!' I scream, heading out the door.

'Don't be back too late!' she replies. I head off. I was informed of a demon rampage, killing several people in my local area. Lucky I don't have to travel or I would have to bother my mom and she would not be happy.

I walk into the warehouse. The poor guys who work through the night, the demon got to them. R.I.P. I walk into the main area and spot 'him' after taking an innocent person as his vessel. The vessel is covered in blood. The victim spread out all over the floor.

'You BA… bad word I'm not allowed to say! Thanks mam!' He laughs.

'So you've finally arrived.' It annoys me how he knew I would turn up, but he continues. 'I had wanted to meet you.' His eyes changed to a soulless black. Evil is evident on his face, even without the blood soaked outfit. It seems as if the soul of the vessel is still inside trying to break out. This is the worst because you have to kill the human as well as the demon.

I reach for my knife in my left boot, the only thing that will kill him without getting really messy. 'Let's hustle!' he shouts. I set off on this dangerous mission.

I have no special powers or anything, just the skills I have acquired in my training. I swerve away from a punch that would have knocked me off my feet and across the room. I kick him in the gut and prepare to stab him in the heart with the knife. He struggles, but I succeed. He screams aloud as his eyes light up from the magical knife. It is quite messy work but it pays off.

I look at my watch. 9:15. Crap! I sprint home for half nine. I arrive home at 9:35. Mother is standing at the door… Waiting to yell.

'Mom, I'm sorry! I got delayed' I say. 'Hmm…' is all she replies as she enters the house. I run upstairs and have a shower. I normally do after a job, maybe washing the sins away.

***

I arise early next morning to get ready for school. It's like I have two lives. During the day I spend it doing math with Miss Lake's 4th graders and at night I fight the supernatural crimes. I grab my lunch and head off to English and then Drama class, like all the regular nine year olds. Boring class.

At lunch I sit on my own. Nobody really understands me. I either plan for the next quest or listen to music on my iPod. 'Panic! At the Disco' all the way! People laugh at me when I walk by or begin to talk about me really loudly to ensure I hear. If you haven't guessed it yet. I HATE school!

I used to love going home after school and joking about with my dad. We would pass a ball as he would tell me stories of interesting or scary experiences he had while working. I used to be worried constantly when he was out. When he went out on that horrific day, I knew something had happened, something really bad. I would remember the close calls he previously had and it would just worry me even more.

Like when he went out with another hunter who was meant to have his back and he got shot in the shoulder by a vampire. Who knew vampires had guns? Or the time he set out to kill a shapeshifter and misjudged their powers. Yet I still felt worried. Terrified. It's hard though, with leviathans, you never know what you are going to get or generally how strong they are.

When I get home my mother tells me a distressed young woman called looking for me. She tells me she left her number and that it is on the notepad beside the phone in the hall. I walk out to the hall and on the tall mahogany table sat the yellow sticky note that reads:

Louise Oakley
Cleveland
557 1294
Call back ASAP!!!

I see the note and I immediately pick up the house phone and dial the number. It takes a few rings for her to answer. It gives me time to think. I use the house phone for obvious reasons. I'm nine! I don't have a cell phone. I wish I did but Mom won't budge.

As Mother said, a distressed women answered.

'Hello? Hello? Hello? Who's this? Why are you calling me?'

'Hi, I'm Charlie Matthews; you left a message with my mother earlier. I rang back as soon as I could,' I reply.

'Oh yes, yes. Please help. I hear things. Vicious dogs growling. They are coming to get me. Please, this is no joke. Please. Please help me.'

'Tell me your address.'

'Isn't that near the crossroads?' Then it all made sense. 'Stay inside! I'll be right over!' I scream down the phone. I hang up and run into Mom. 'Please drive me to her house now! It's about a deal!'

In the car on the way there I have time to think. Deals are tricky business. You basically sell your soul to a demon for something they will give you. You will be happy; you kiss the demon to seal the deal. (Yuk!) But there is a consequence, ten years after the deal is made the demon's hell hounds come and kill you to take your soul. A very idiotic decision but usually the victims don't entirely understand the implications at hand or they are really desperate.

***

I run up to her house and I bang on the door. As I stand there waiting I hear several bolts unlocking and chains moving above the key hole. Finally I hear the door handle rattle and Louise appears. Her long blond hair is tied back away from her face. Her bangs are pinned to the side and she dresses for comfort, baggy sweatpants and a loose tee.

'Please come in,' she said first of all. I can tell from her voice it is not a suggestion, it is a demand. She isn't going to stay outside for long. I knew the hounds were near. She locks the door and we head further into the house, Mom following closely behind.

First I cover any areas near doors and windows with salt. Demons and hell hounds cannot work with salt. I also make a generous circle in the centre of the room for Louise to stand in.

I draw symbols around the room repelling any demon entity from entering the house as well. This works most of the time; you just have to be careful where you put them.

Louise soon informs me of scratching on the door. Her face grows pale, almost transparent. Her heart races to a rapid pace.

Soon the scratches become louder, loud enough that I can now hear them. I know that action is close. I prepare with a gun loaded with demon trap-encrusted bullets and my 'magical' demon killing knife (also works on hell hounds), the only thing that can truly kill a demon and send them back to hell.

The scratching has evolved to a banging against the door. It's my time to shine. I burst out of the door.

I hear growling surrounding me. It appears suddenly, and then disappears again. I know where it is now. I set forward on this dangerous endeavour.

The growls get more defined as I near the hound. I stab my arm forward, knife in hand and hope it works. I'm worried as I'm so in-experienced with this breed of 'dog'. I stab again, my heart racing, fear in my eyes. This might be the last chance I get before it fights back.

It begins to howl. 'Got cha!' I stab again to ensure it is dead. How ironic, in a movie people are generally more sad over the death of an animal but in these terms people may be overjoyed with the outcome. While this thought appears in my mind I head inside.

I ask an important question... 'You only made one deal, right?' Louise replies with a definite yes. Relieved, I encourage her not to make anymore. After tidying up, mom and I say our goodbyes and head off home, exhausted. After that experience I am surprisingly sleepy, and nod off on the drive home – which I never do.

***

My mom let me have the next day off. So I go into school today 're-freshed and ready to work'. I think those were the words she used. Any-how I set off to Miss Lake's room, Room 111 for the best class to start the day... Maths! (I assure you I'm joking!)

At lunch I set off to a secluded table to read a novel I had found in the library, the book talks about vampires and demons. As I sit there I laugh at how incorrect the information is. HA! HA! Vampires, can't bear sunlight? HA! People are completely oblivious to the fact that vampires walk among us whether the sun is splitting the skies or not.

I hear a loud BANG out in the hallway. I go to check it out. Stopping dead in my tracks, I see the 'King' of Hell standing there. The worst demon known to any hunter, Mathekin, is in my school. You know you are in trouble when Mathekin, King of Hell is in your school, most likely looking for you.

'Crap!' I scream. I think I know the demon that Louise made the deal with. 'Real smart Louise'. People look at me strangely now as I start yelling random sentences out loud. People begin whispering again.

'What the hell is she doing?'

'Wow, she's so stupid.'

'Honestly, will you just leave?' Who knew nine year olds knew such bad language? Some people need to learn to whisper?!?!

'Why did you come here?' I say, speaking directly to Mathekin. He laughs loudly, pushing past people as he begins to walk nearer to me. 'Retribution must be made since you killed my beloved hound. I thought he had something special', He wipes away an imaginary tear. 'Oh well,' a smile reappears on his face. He is almost giggling.

'What now?' I look at him with despair.

'Now, we fight!' he said smirking. 'To the death...' he said slowly. It gave me a chill through-out my body. Hairs stand up on the back of my neck. He continues, 'You kill my dog, I kill you!'

'As if!' Worry now builds up, making me feel nauseous. 'I'm only nine!' keeps racing through my mind. 'You have powers, that's an advantage! How is that fair?'

'Strictly fighting, is that better?'

'I suppose. Can I have a minute to breathe?'

'You didn't give Lucifer a minute to breathe...'

'What?' I must have looked really confused.

'My dog... Lucifer...'

'Oh, well sorry.' Lie.

'Fine then, if you must.'

'Thank you. Please wait outside. I don't want to wreck this horrible school.' Never thought I'd say that.

**

One. Two. Three. Breathe Anna, breathe. I will be okay, it will be okay! I consider running away but that would leave everyone in danger. It is my fault. It is my duty to do this. I start walking through the now empty corridors. I make my way to the door and I see the horrid creature standing alone on the grass of the football fields.

As I stand on the grass, I notice people staring out the window of their classrooms. Pressure is on, as all their eyes stare down on me. I face Mathekin now. A bead of sweat drips down my face from my eyebrow, my heart literally in my throat as he begins to talk about starting. It's nice of him to give me some time. I laugh loudly as he observes me.

Out of nowhere as if he was in my brain, he pounces, catching me off guard. Luckily I am prepared. My knife slips down my sleeve and is now tightly being gripped by my sweaty hands. The fight is on. 'Rocky' music plays in my head.

I keep light on my toes and constantly moving on my feet. I cover as much of my body as I can with my arms, placed in a fighting position. For once I feel silly fighting an adult but what can I do... I have no choice.

As Mathekin moves around me in a circular motion, I prepare my hand to stab forward at any chance I get. His eyes avert onto the students in the windows for a split second and I stab forward. I miss. Crap! Without thinking he comes back from the daze, knife in hand also ready to stab forward.

I try again. Miss. One last try. 'This is for everyone I saved!' The knife plunges into the heart. Blood begins to flow out of the incision. I hear cackling. The realisation hits me. Pain overwhelms me. The ground nears me and I fall. I end up on the floor like a pile of clothes on the ground.

As I take my last breaths, I think of my mother. When was the last time I told her I loved her? My father. I now know how he felt, but is my passing really worthwhile? Soon enough, everything blanks out. My father is the last thought in my mind. I never felt true love. I never got kissed. I never grew up and got married but one thing I am glad about is that I never had children. Who would want to live in my shadow, and to go through something like this?

Crash

Alex O'Dea

The car was crumpled against the tree. The bonnet was now wrapped around the trunk. Windscreen shattered everywhere into tiny little diamonds. The car crushed against the tree so easily, yet the tree seemed completely unharmed. The driver lay unconscious against the inflated air bags, covered in blood.

I sneak into the office, late again. A few of the people around my cubicle give me dirty looks, but most do not notice.

"Oh good you're here!" my boss says peeking his head out of his office.

"Yeah, sorry sir, I-" I try to think of an excuse but before I can he interrupts me.

"Can you join me in my office for a moment?" he asks. I follow him in.

"Have a seat," he says gesturing towards the chair. I feel a huge knot form in my stomach.

"So, Harry, em, you've been working here for…?" He asks.

"Em, around three months," I reply.

"Yeah and I think we can both agree your work performance hasn't been up to standards. I mean I talked to you just last month about it. But I haven't seen any changes-" he explains.

"I know sir. I'm sorry, I truly am. It's just a lot has been going on at home. I promise that from here on out it'll be different," I scramble for words, trying to think of any plausible excuses. I'm definitely going to need a drink after this conversation.

"Look, Harry, this sounds like a rerun of last month's meeting. I'm afraid we're going to have to let you go," he says.

"Oh. Okay. Yeah Okay," I stutter.

"Take your time clearing out your things." he says as I leave his office. I walk straight to my desk, being very careful not to make eye contact with any of my coworkers. I am too embarrassed to face them and their 'sympathetic' looks. All I can think about is my daughter, Lydia, and how I have let her down again. I can't even bear the thought of telling her that I have lost another job. The mere idea of it makes me feel ill. The only thing that can make this situation any less depressing is going to the pub. So I collect my few possessions. I need to get out of here as quickly as possible. I throw my things into the back of my car and drive off to the nearest bar.

Several hours later I have to leave the bar, the staff say they have to stop serving me. I stumble out into the pouring rain and after pointing my keys at the wrong car for a while I finally find my car and drive off.

The door slam echoes through the near silent hall and brings everyone's attention to Sheila, the secretary, who walks with her head down up to the front of the room. She whispers something into the professor's ear.

"Lydia Phillips?" he calls

"Eh, yeah?" I raise my hand.

"There's an urgent message for you at the office, you're excused." he says.

I have never been more thankful to be excused from a lecture, it was the most boring one that I have been to all year. I grab my things and dash for the door. Sheila was standing there waiting for me. She gives me a sympathetic look and reaches for my arm as we walk out of the room.

"Dear, I'm afraid I have some bad news," she says. My heart begins to race.

"The police just rang the school looking for you, they said to pass on the message that your father has been in a car accident, apparently his car hit a tree. He's at Beaumont Hospital now, they're looking after him. They said he's in quite critical condition. I am so sorry sweetie," she says.

"Oh. My. God. Oh my god. I think I'm gonna be sick," I mumble while clutching my stomach.

"Is there anything I can do, dear?" she asks as I jog off.

"No, I have to go!" I respond.

"Thank you though! I'm sorry!" I shout back when I am halfway down the hall.

I run out of the school to my car in the parking lot. I can hardly think straight. My thoughts are mostly just a blur and my heart is pounding in my chest. I start thinking of my dad lying in a hospital bed and next thing I know my eyes are filling with tears and they start streaming down my cheeks. I start to lose control of my breathing and I have to pullover to catch it again and to wipe my eyes. He'll be fine. Don't worry. He'll be fine. His car just hit a tree, how much damage could have even been done?

How did he even manage to hit a tree? He's generally a good driver, that is, when he's not drunk. Oh my god. I bet he was drunk! How else could someone crash into a tree in broad daylight? He's so irresponsible it's ridiculous. I feel like I'm the adult in the house most of the time. I can't believe this is actually happening. If he was drunk I am actually going to kill him. How could he be so reckless? He's the only family I have, I don't know how I'd manage without him. I can't help but think it wasn't entirely an accident. I can't even let myself think like that. But it is a strong possibility. He hasn't been the same since Mam left. He has lost like three jobs in the past two years. He's just not really all there anymore. To think that it could have been a suicide attempt. My tears start to build back up again. I hope, above everything else, that it was an accident. I don't think that I could handle knowing that my own father tried to take his life, the thought is sickening. I need him so much more than he knows; he is one of the most important people in my life.

So I need to pull myself together and be there for him. I manage to calm myself enough to stop crying and I drive off to the hospital.

Everything's been going wrong today. I just want my shift to be over. Working for the past eleven hours. I'm exhausted. I just want to go home and sleep. Another call, someone has driven into a tree. And we're off to the scene of the accident. Once we arrive everyone's rushing about. The fire brigade are cutting the driver out of the car. Brian and I are leaning against the back of the ambulance. The stretcher is at our feet. We wait 'til we're called. I stand there watching everyone. There are at least ten people here, all to help this one man. Every one of them looks stressed and exhausted. The driver is unconscious, with blood covering most of his body. He seems so limp and lifeless. Seeing people in such a state has a way of sticking in your mind. It always comes back to haunt you. Each accident like this has left such an impact on me and I'm guessing my coworkers too, although we have never actually talked about it. This one man has caused so much chaos. I can't imagine how worrying it is to get a call saying that your loved one has been in a crash. Even just looking at the crash I can tell it was easily avoidable. No sign of a skid or anything like that. If this man had been more careful all of these things could have been avoided. Everything would be fine. The complete idiot! We have dealt with many accidents like this before. But I have never put that much thought into it.

"You ready? Looks like they've got him out now," Brian says to me, picking up his end of the stretcher.

"Yeah, go on," I pick up my half and head towards the car.

We place him very gently on the stretcher and jog quickly and carefully to the ambulance. Once he is placed safely in the ambulance, we take off. We are doing everything we can to keep him alive. We don't have a second to breathe. We are constantly tending to him. It is such a relief when we get to the hospital and the doctors take him out of our hands. As I watch the stretcher being wheeled through the door I begin to feel almost guilty for what I had thought. I know nothing about him. For all I know this crash could have been purely an accident. But I think the main reason that I feel guilty is that I am unsure whether he will even make it through the night.

Destroying My Past
Adam O'Rourke

After being distracted from over-thinking and daydreaming I realized I had finished my cigarette. I got the butt of the smoke and flicked it away with my index finger not caring where it would end up. After, I started shuffling my feet up to Wispy. I was just a normal sixteen year old who did things. Sure why should I care I was brought up to not care about anything or anyone. Even smoking has always been a part of my life. People have said to me about giving it up but how could you when your father buys you packets of smokes! We even go halves on the cigarettes the odd time!

As I reached Wispy with the remaining toxins floating out of my mouth I put on my jacket and me and Wispy were on our way home.

"It's Baltic out isn't it John?" Wispy said zipping up his coat.

"I know yeah me fee' are frozen they are!"

"Ye up for a fifa tournament, I'll give the lads a buzz."

"I had it last time, so you can have one this time Wispy!"

"Alrigh' relax Johno I'll see, I'll see!"

"Gudman Wispy, will I bring a few cold ones?"

"Yeah alrigh', only a few pal."

"Nice one Wispy I'll see ye tonight then yeah?"

"Righ' nice one."

After talking about rubbish Wispy and I had one more smoke before we went home. When I was dragging my feet down the path just after finishing that smoke I looked up at my chimney, it was huffing and puffing like my father after his five minute jog in the morning. I walked up to my door and I looked in the small window. I couldn't see much, well how could you with a window that has layers of dirt resting on both sides. When I got to my door, I took out my key and slotted it smoothly into the lock and I pushed the door open silently.

"Dad? You home?" I said slowly walking towards the basement where the music was coming from.

Just as I was about to push open the basement door, I could hear the sound of someone sprinting up the old damp wooden stairs. I was met by my father peeping his head out of the room, he had sweat pouring down his face and his hair looking like it just got 100 thousand volts of electricity ran through it. There was an awkward silence between us, neither of us knew what to say.

"Da, what are ye doin' in there?"

"Ehmm... I'm just workin' ou' son! I'll be up in a sec! Get your oul fella a fresh box of fags will ye?" he stuttered every word.

"Alrigh', nice one Da," I said trying to have a sneaky look in the room.

As I was walking away I took a sneaky look behind me, I couldn't believe it. It looked like there was crystal meth in these square boxes, I stopped and looked behind me. With all my anger I ran at the door punching and kicking the door violently.

"Da what are you doing!" I said in a rage.

"One sec son," he said.

I kept going, suddenly I could hear the latch starting to loosen up, I went even harder and harder!

"Son I'm coming now, will ye stop!" he said, making his way up the stairs.

I just kept going, my anger had taken control of me. To my surprise the door of the basement flew against the wall, although that wasn't the only thing that broke,

Just as I opened the door my father got a smack of the door, which sent him tumbling down the stairs.

When I looked down the stairs, my father was flat out on the solid concrete floor, lying there with a pool of blood seeping through the crack in his skull and blood dripping off the edge of the table. I looked at him. I couldn't believe it!

"Son...son," he whispered, using all the energy left in his body.

I ran down the stairs. Quickly I ran over to his side and knelt beside him.

"Take this son..." he handed me a piece of paper with numbers and letters on it.

When I examined the paper, it looked to be some chemical formula, I didn't really care, there wasn't enough time to care. I stuffed the formula into the side of my Nike Airmax and quickly turned back to listen to my father.

"Just keep it safe son, time will tell when you will need it, I'm terribly sorry," he said with his dying breath.

That was it! He was gone, I looked down at him. I was in shock, I couldn't believe it. I took my phone out of my jacket, and I dialled the police.

"Send an ambulance to 34 Springdale and also send the DS (drug squad) thanks."

I dropped the phone and slid down the wall, I put my hands onto my face and wept myself to sleep.

***

I woke up knowing this was my last day, I was out to face the world on my own.

"You ready, John?" I heard coming from the door.

"Yeah one sec, just give me 5 minutes alone, thanks," I said looking at her in despair.

I looked around the room. I wondered how many things I had broken in this room, it's hard to imagine how many times I had woken up screaming. The nightmare was always the same, the day my father died. For over 2 years I had seen that night, there was nothing I could do to stop it. I used to hate sleeping I would rather run through the hot ashes to know I'd sleep knowing I didn't have to go through that torture for another night.

"John it's time to go," she said looking at me trying to give me a hopeful smile.

I picked up my bags, I looked one last time hoping to get rid of the old and in with the new. As I was leaving, there were so many people to wave me off, I know nearly every single person in the home, sure each person had to deal with me at least once or twice. I was just uncontrollable, there were issues that had never been dealt with properly.

As I was leaving the building you would know they would say

"Come back soon!" or "good luck out there!"

But the people in there don't care, for five minutes they would be like

"Ahh bless him," or "the poor young fella."

Then after the fake tears and the fake opinions they would laugh about the child who's so messed up, who can barely tie his own shoes.

"John!.. John! Are you even listening to me?."

"Oh sorry I was day dreaming Chantelle."

"Right then! I'll explain it again, we have set up a job for you in the city it's not too bad, we are renting an apartment for you for the first six months. Then it's up to you John!" She said trying to stay positive.

"Thanks," I said picking up my bags.

As she hugged me and said her final goodbyes, she strolled back into work waving me one last hopeful goodbye. There always was that person who actually cared about you and you could always rely on, and that was her - the only real person in the foster home.

Without realizing the bus had pulled up at the bus stop.

"You gettin' on or wha' buddy?"

I hopped on and put the 2 euro down the machine, I took my seat just behind the driver's seat. Just as the door was closing, it was interrupted by a woman. As she lazily put her glasses on her forehead gently, she looked at the bus driver in a rude manor. She put the glasses back over her small eyes and she put the shiny euro down the machine. This woman was wearing a very long black coat, she had jet black Ray Bans, even though it was a very gloomy day. She looked old but you could see she was trying her best to keep herself looking well. She walked up the bus in her shiny leather black boots. She stopped. She looked down. She took the seat beside me. I didn't really mind because she seemed like an intriguing woman. As she turned around looking straight at my face, she took off her overpriced Ray Bans, she flicked her short light blonde to the right hand side. I looked away, making it look like I didn't know she was looking at me, but what came next I could not believe!

"Hi, John," she said very seriously.

My heart sank into my stomach hoping that I wouldn't be sucked into my past. I turned around facing her trying to put on a serious face but I was crumbling inside.

'How do you know my name?' I said stuttering.

"I'm your mother, John," she said.

No you're not my mother, she died at birth, prove it if you say you are! I said smirking to myself.

"You have a small little birth mark on your top right shoulder, it is brown and also very clear, you also lived with your father and when he died, you went to a foster home for two years," she said very convincingly.

I couldn't believe what I just heard, I must have been dreaming this had to be impossible. But that fear and the cheeky laugh awoke a fury inside me that had been building up for over two years and it was finally about to spill over.

In rage I slammed down the stop button, I went over to the doors and left just as the bus stopped.

"John come back! Just let me explain!" My mother roared at me getting out of the bus.

When I left the bus I just started running up the road trying to get rid of my past. But your past always catches up with you, as I turned the corner I was met by three Guards there ready to grab me like I was a piece off meat of the plate of Christmas dinner. So I stood there instead of trying to run away, they grabbed me and dragged me into the back of a squad car. They threw me in and locked the door behind me.

"This is an absolute joke, let me out of here, I've not done anything!" I said trying to open the door.

I was met by my so-called mother opening the back door.

"You get outa' here! You're pretending to be me mother when you're not! She died at childbirth! Now leave me alone before I stab you in the throat you psycho!"

As she took her seat there was a terrifying silence between us, I didn't know what to say.

"John, your father was one of the best crystal meth producers in all of Europe, I was in love with him, I loved everything about him, well until I saw him making his blue stuff, as they call it on the streets. I didn't know what to do because I am head of the drug squad so it was the most horrible time of my life, the decisions that I had to make were the most challenging decisions I've ever had to make in my life, John," she said.

I had calmed down a small bit I was still really unsure though, but I got comfortable.

"What did you do after you found out about the meth?" I asked, hoping that she was actually my mother.

"Well after I found out I made the decision to have the baby and then fake my death."

As the anger was almost starting to boil up in my body again I looked sharply into her eyes and said, "Why didn't you ever come see me?"

"I was going to see you, I was going to give you the life that you had deserved!" she said sliding onto the seat beside me.

"Then why didn't you see me? Why didn't you?" I said, interrupting her.

"You interrupted our drug bust John!" she shouted me.

"It's my fault is it Mam? You expect me to just forgive you after the pain and suffering you have caused me, after that foster home you expect me to be OK after all I've been through!" I said wiping the tears flowing down my cheeks.

"No John just give me a chance please! I'm begging you! Just let me help you," she stuttered.

As I looked at her, down on her knees, begging for my forgiveness, I couldn't take anymore pain, I couldn't take the stress, I just wanted to have a good memory in my brain. I looked down.

I said reluctantly, "how will you help me?"

"John you're going to the Irish army"

***

"I'm of Johno! Will you lock up the place?" Conor said with his head hanging out the entrance to the door.

"Ye alrigh', do you have the keys Con?"

"Heads up Johno!" he threw a set of keys through the air.

"Sound Conor, I'll see you after, have a good one bud," I said.

I was leaving the Irish headquarters after finding out I was next to take over as the captain of the Irish army, I was astonished, well it made sense really, I was awarded with several medals from being on the battle field. Sure I was the best you could get, I was in the Irish Army for 5 years, then I served in the British army for another 5 years and now I'm back home, where I belong. I am also the youngest captain at 28, sure even my mother still can't believe how much I've changed. I still kept in contact with my mom, Cindy, she was always in work though, she said she's been saying the past while she has 'someone big.' The girl-friend's name was Bertha, I met her in the Irish army, she was probably the only person who kept me going. After over-thinking and a half an hour drive I finally was at my house, but when I finally pulled up out-side my house, there was something going on, and I didn't like it. I got out of my overpriced car, I walked to my door and slotted my key into the keyhole and pushed the door open silently.

"Hello... Hello!" I said starting to get a bit nervy.

"John."

I spun my head around, I looked at the entrance of the kitchen. I started walking silently but swiftly to the entrance of the kitchen, I put my sweaty hand in my pocket, slowly I took out the gun and aimed at the door. My pores were pouring sweat, me knees were trembling and my heart felt like it was going to jump out of my chest.

"1...2...3" I whispered.

I ran and kicked the door open, I scouted out the room, pointing my gun in front of me all at the same time, I looked at the kitchen table. I was shocked, my mother was sitting there with her right leg crossed over her left one and she was sipping on her steamy cup of tea. I put my gun back into my inside pocket and stood there like a statue.

"Mam...? What are you doing here?"

"John you don't have something that belongs to your father..? Do you?" She looked at me with her raised eyebrows.

"I thought you were leaving for the States today, for some kind of meeting," I said grabbing a chair from underneath the table.

"John remember the day your father died," she said placing the mug on the table.

It was starting to get weird now, why was she asking me all these questions? My family also wasn't here, there was something going on, I could feel it.

"Mam what's wrong?" I said.

"Did he give you anything John, I need to know?" she said seriously.

"I don't think so to be honest, I can't remember."

"John just think!' she said grabbing my face.

Just think! What clothes you were wearing! Did you have anything special on you that day! What shoes, anything!"

I suddenly stepped into my shoes that day, when I thought long and hard it was simple, the answer was in the question!

"Shoes! SHOES!" I screamed

That was it, I looked at her with a serious smile, I sprinted towards the living room, up the stairs, and I ran into my bedroom. I flung open my wardrobe. My mam came running up the stairs after me, she sounded like she had burst a lung. Shoebox after shoebox they were getting flung out of the dresser. I still hadn't found out why I was doing this, but I couldn't stop, I was so caught up in the moment. Not even realizing, there it was the Nike Airmax shoebox lying right there in front of me, when I flicked back the box, there they were. The stereotypical trainers shining under the dim light. The exquisite Nike tick was like eye candy, they had white leather on the front and sides, they were in impeccable condition, the best thing was the inside, every time you put them on you would think you're in heaven, they were just amazing.

"Where is it John?" she whispered.

I reached my hand into the two shoes, I could feel a piece of paper in the right shoe, I slipped it into my fingers and pulled it out quickly. Just as I started analysing the information, a hand quickly pulled it from my grasp.

"Hey!" I said getting to my feet.

"Look John, it's for your own good," she said walking out the door.

"Mam wait! What's out of my hands?!" I said shouting at her.

"John someone's taken your family hostage, OK!"

"What…"

I felt sick, I couldn't believe it, and I felt like I was responsible, I had to make amends. I walked downstairs struggling to keep my body stable, I walked into the kitchen where my mother was.

"What do I have to do?"

***

Just as my mother was about to speak, her iPhone started vibrating. She looked at me in horror, she was shuffling around in her pocket searching for the phone, when she finally got it, she took it out, and placed it gently to her ear.

"Hello," She said softly.

"Dear, you do realise you have ten minutes left to get what I asked for, or do have to kill this woman?"

"Yes I do have it you psycho-maniac fool, I swear to god when I get my hands on you I'm going to tear every single one of your bones out! Feed them to a pack of starving wolves I will!" she said shaking with anger.

"Cindy you do realize what's at stake here, don't you? So how's your boy holding up? I'm messing, I'm sure he's alright, anyways meet me up in Reileys Hill, the deal will take place in four hours. Then we can get back to old ways, you chasing me around, I'll keep running, because Cindy, I know I'll never get caught dear."

She took the phone slowly away from her ear, she looked horrified, but that face had gone from horror to anger, she dialled in another number and put the phone to her ear.

"Send everyone in now, I'm not letting him slip through my fingers again!" she said.

"John clear the table, turn on the kettle, and get ready."

"I'll put the army on standby," I said moving the chairs away from the table.

"Don't it will cause too much attention, trust me, I don't need that right now," she said taking a map out of her pocket and folding it out onto the table.

Just as I was about to reply the living room shone up, two headlights were shining through the glass window, when I looked out the window, another car came, then another, then another one after one they kept coming. People who looked like James Bond were getting out of each car, each person was walking right through my front door. The men all looked the exact same, had the same build, showed no emotion, and all had the slick back hairstyle. Before I knew it, my house had become the new headquarters for the drug squad.

"John cup of tea now" My mother said in the mist of the dementors.

After two hours and 6 cups of tea, the plan was ready.

"John get over here!" I heard from the table.

When I walked over, my mother was giving orders.

"John you go in to do the deal, I'm sorry, he specifically asked you," she whimpered.

"Right get your guns ready, take your positions, the mission is a go!" she said drastically.

Just before I left she hugged me. When I was getting in my car, I realized, I couldn't follow the plan, my odds were poor and so were Berthas, my main priority was my Bertha. It was time to stop my past catching up with me, I couldn't let anyone I got close to be the consequence for my mistakes. When I looked through my windscreen my mother was distracted, this was my chance to do this, quickly I stepped out of my car, I tip toed silently but swiftly into the kitchen, stepping by all the dementors. I needed to find my mothers jacket, her jacket was Bertha's key to freedom, from the corner of my eye, I saw it on the kitchen table, I walked over to it, this was it I couldn't get this wrong, or it was game over. I looked around quickly and went for it, I checked the right pocket, I pulled out everything it wasn't there. Suddenly I heard my mother giving orders, she was close I had to act fast. I ruffled around her left pocket, I felt the piece of paper, I took it, and slipped it into my back pocket quickly. Just as I was leaving the kitchen, she walked in.

"John c'mon everyone is leaving!" she said power-walking over towards her jacket.

I quickly ran over to my car, and I got in, I needed to leave before my mother realized what I done, I turned on my new Mercedes Benz engine, I was out of my house quicker than a thief. Just as I was leaving, I took one last look at my house. It could be the last time I would see the house after all, but I was met by mothers face shining under the dim porch light, she was looking right at me with a smile, but it wasn't just a smile, it was a smile as if the battle had been already won. I didn't really know what she was trying to tell me or if she was just happy, but trust me she never is. I didn't think about it, my mind was already racing with a hundred different thoughts and possibilities. I set my GPS to Reilly's Hill, I was still on track, but I needed to get there ahead of the drug squad. When no one was looking, I took a sharp left and hid in a little ally way, one by one the cars were passing by the alleyway. This was my chance, I set a marker on the back roads, and I was on my way.

***

When I reached my destination, I realized why this was the place, no satellite signal, it was the middle of nowhere, It was simply perfect for a drug dealer. When I looked around the corner, the entrance was there right in front of me, there was a foggy mist creeping up the hill. The path looked endless, and I didn't like it, I got out of my car suspiciously, I closed the door behind me. When I reached the gate, I was met with a vile stench which I could almost taste. I entered the dark place, I took out my gun, and I was ready for anything or anyone. I reached the middle of the path, the smell was getting stronger and I was starting to get a bit light headed. Suddenly, I heard what seemed footsteps running around, they were advancing on me at every second, I had to act, but there was simply nowhere to go, they were getting closer and closer! Everywhere I went my face was getting torn by sharp thorns, I couldn't see, the fog was everywhere, I had to stand my ground.

"CRACKLE" I heard from directly behind me.

"Hello!" I said standing like a statue.

"Shouldn't have come here buddy," a cold voice whispered in my ear.

Just as I was turning around, a baseball bat that hit me right in the jaw and almost made my head do a full spin. I fell to the floor with my face seeping blood, my eyes half shut, and my ears buzzing like a bee, but a kick to my head completed the job, I was out cold for now.

***

"Wake up!"

Someone was shouting in my face, I didn't really care, I was completely out of the real world at this moment in time. I was awoken abruptly when a rough hand hit me across my jaw, I was awake now, but I just remembered where I was.

"AGHHHH," I screamed out in shock.

"Goodman, your awake now, d'ya have de' formula buddy!?" He said angrily.

When I got my bearings, I looked up, I saw a man who had runners which were ready for the dump, he was wearing a full Nike tracksuit, his face was in a terrible state, he had a scar right down the side of his neck, It was most definitely infected, and finally his face had terrible potholes from what seemed to be acne. That wasn't the worst part though, his breath had a taste of sour milk with a mixture of nail polish remover. It made me physically sick! When I looked around, I couldn't see much, just a lot of men and many parked SUV's around a small little fire.

"Buddy WHERES THE FORMULA!" he said putting his dirty hands

on my neck ready to pull my guts from inside me.

"One sec!" I said

I reached for my pockets to take out the piece of paper, I couldn't find it. I checked everywhere it definitely wasn't there.

"No no!" I said panicking on the chair.

"Of course, your old hag lets me down again, Bring her out!" he said

When I looked over, I saw my wife come out from behind a tree. She was in a mess.   She was strapped to a wheelie chair she had blood all over her face, her hair looked like she had been dragged through tar, her clothes were ripped to shreds. It was like as if she was fed to a pack of animals! It was horrible.

"What have you done?!" I looked in agonising pain.

"Ah sure, desperate times call for desperate measures," he said walking over to my wife taking out his revolver from his pocket.

"Stop I'll do anything! Please!" I said trying my best to get free.

He clipped the gun back, and he pointed it at Bertha, he looked back at me with an evil smile and said,

"Say your last words!"

I shut my eyes, I couldn't even look.

"BANGGGG!"

I couldn't believe it, I might as well just have died on the spot, I couldn't look at the mess. It was my entire fault, I was still the person I had been after my father died. A weak sixteen year old child.

"Everyone take your positions!" someone said.

When I heard those words, there was a glimmer of hope. When I forced myself to look up, the dealer was on the floor half conscious with blood pouring from his arm. Bertha was still alive, I got another chance to make everything right. But not for long, there were bullets going from one side to another of the forest and Bertha and I were in the middle of it. I had to act fast. I saw a knife sticking out of the dealer's jacket and I reached inside and took it out. I was cutting the rope. Suddenly a whistling bullet flew into the side of my leg, the sound of my flesh spluttering the blood like a hose was immense. I barely felt it, my adrenalin was racing through my body. When I got free I jumped to the ground. I heard were the bullets flying over my head and the screeches coming from the men getting shot. I reached Bertha but just as I was about to cut her free, I seen a shadow coming from behind me, I turned around and he was ready to squash me like a bug. When he tried to stand on my head I jabbed him in the sole of the foot and he let off a squeal and he fell on his face. When I saw his face it was there leader, his breath still reeked of milk even though his mouth was had blood stringing down his crusty lips, but this time he was even more scary looking. I was right beside Bertha, I just needed to get her out of the hot zone. I pushed the chair and it was in the dark no one could see her, she was safe, but I wasn't. I was met with a solid fist to the face, I turned back around but it wasn't just one, he just kept going, I was barely functioning, my body and my mind was shutting down, and I was loosing to much blood, I had to act fast or I was finished. I blocked one of the punches and loafed him right in his nose, the noise of his bone splitting in two was a relief but also wasn't nice at the same time.

"C'mon you scumbag!" I said getting to my barely functional legs.

Every punch I was blocking, and hitting him square in the nose, it was immense, I lost nearly every battle in my life, there's was no chance I was going to loose the greatest battle of them all though. He finally fell, and so did his crew, the gunfire stopped, the men in black won, and I had completed my mission. Keeping Bertha alive.

***

It was great waking up I had no problems anymore I had defeated my past and I was where I was meant to be, I seen my mother all the time, she was retired as the drug squad chief and I was still head of the army, I had two kids of my own and I was married now to Bertha. The dealers name was Chico in the end and he went to prison for life and so did his "friends". One thing I couldn't forget was the nightmare, that was never going to be forgotten or it was never going to be erased from my stone cold memory. There was nothing that could change that, or no one that could help me. One thing I did know for sure, I never had to worry about sleeping anymore. I was miles ahead of the nightmare.

Decay

Hazel O'Shea

It was a small settlement; four rows of cabins sat in the shadow of the factory, silver vine-like plants snaking their way around them, entwined around the fence which marked the perimeter. Patches of the standard blue paint could still be seen on the walls, but mostly it was peeling or had faded to a dull grey.

Everywhere they looked was grey, as though the planet had been tipped over and all the colour had trickled out. Despite their weathered appearances, the buildings seemed mostly intact, with one notable exception.

The smokestacks, like trees uprooted in a storm, were tilted at an improbable angle, suffocating under the iron grip of the vines. These vines spewed out from the mostly collapsed roof and flowed out over the crumbling walls onto the sprawling undergrowth below. Yet it was still an imposing structure, and she felt drawn to it.

"This is where the signal is coming from?"

Ellory shrugged. "I think so. But it's not our job to find out. We should go back to the ship and get this patrol over with. You can report it when we get back."

The beginnings of irritation began to gnaw at her. How she managed to always get saddled with him, her brother of all people, on these patrols she would never understand. She ducked down, and stepped through the gap in the fence.

"What is with you? Are you seriously that afraid to break a few rules?"

"Yes, actually." He said, kicking an errant stone at his feet.

She turned back toward the settlement, feeling the strange draw towards it more strongly than before.

"You really need to lighten up." With that, she stalked forward, Ellory trailing behind after a few moments, muttering complaints under his breath.

The main hall was almost cavernous. Boarded up windows lined the walls, gloomy light filtering in through the gaps. Dust seemed to coat every surface, the few pieces of furniture rotting where they stood.

Small patches of colour on the far wall caught her eye and she drifted over, leaving Ellory by the entrance, fiddling with equipment as he hummed tunelessly. She ran her fingers over the drawings, the wobbly lines etched into the cracking plaster of the walls. They were childlike in their simplicity and exaggerated proportions; depictions of the moons and stars, the cabins outside, faces with big smiles but sad eyes. She looked back toward Ellory, who was staring into space, perplexed.

"Is there something wrong?"

"No, no. I just...I don't know. Déjà vu maybe." He shrugged, but continued to stare at the wall bemusedly.

"You know where the broadcast is coming from, right?" She asked, peering over his shoulder to look at the screen.

"I'm not sure. The co-ordinates keep fluctuating."

"Don't worry Ellory. We'll find it in no time!"

Another dead-end.

She slumped against the wall.

"We should have turned left that time."

"If I remember correctly, I had said as such at the time. The readings said we were-"

"Ellory, the readings said we were close about two hours ago. And they said we were close when we ended up in the basement, and when we were stuck in that supply closet. Seriously, there must be something wrong with that thing."

"It is functioning perfectly, and besides, if we had continued our routine patrol instead of gallivanting down here, chasing after some random distress signal, we wouldn't be in this situation now, would we?"

"I'm sorry, but I didn't force you to come with me, I told you that you could stay on the ship."

"Right, like I would let you go wandering off into some creepy settlement by yourself." He turned to go back the way they came, but stopped when he saw she hadn't moved. She cleared her throat. He waited for her to speak.

"Ellory, why did you really come? If you really didn't want to be here, you would have stayed behind, or more than likely dragged me back to the ship."

He sighed, looking everywhere but directly at her.

"I don't know, I guess it was just so nice to see you interested in something. Just, being yourself again. I felt like it was worth getting in trouble later."

"Oh." It was all she could think to say.

She contemplated telling him everything; the memory loss, the whispering voices and the tinny laugh that would ring in her ears for hours on end, the times she had woken up somewhere hours from base covered in cuts and bruises, with no memory of how she got there. How sometimes she wondered if she was even in control of her own body or mind.

Ellory was watching her, concern obvious on his face. She wanted to tell him. But, she couldn't. Not yet.

"I've been really tired, and I wasn't feeling well and, uh, you know how it is. But I'm fine now, really."

Ellory looked far from convinced. She didn't blame him, but was relieved when he dropped the subject.

They had been winding their way through the labyrinth of corridors and passages for nearly an hour when they reached an oblong room, running along the length of a courtyard. Ellory set to the task of getting rid of the pile of rubble blocking the doorway at the other end of the room, convinced that they would find the source beyond it. Neither had spoken the whole way there; Ellory had seemed to be deep in thought and she was just glad he wasn't asking any more questions.

She paced back and forth as she waited, but the silence became too stifling for her to bear.

"I'm just going to go out into the courtyard. I need some air."

Ellory mumbled something in response as she stepped outside.

The courtyard was crowned with an overhanging of silver, light streaming down through tiny gaps in the vine canopy onto the flagstone floor. Small piles of rubble, mostly cracked slates, were dotted haphazardly around the yard. It was dominated by a large mirror, the frame fringed with silver leaf. As she approached, a mass of whitish curls caught her eye. She froze.

A child, wearing a uniform similar to her own, but with hair past her waist, stood to the right of her reflection. The girl had no features on her face, just smooth silvery white skin, and dark voids where eyes should have been. The familiar feeling of fear and euphoria chilled her bones. But she couldn't look away. She became aware of a faint murmur of whispering voices in the distance that seemed to increase in volume and pitch as the seconds went by, until it felt as if they were screaming in her ears. She could feel her legs moving, closer and closer to the mirror.

Ellory called out to her.

"I got that door open!"

Suddenly the voices were gone, and she was gasping for breath, her worried reflection alone staring back at her. She turned away from the mirror, trying to control her panic as she walked back inside. She headed straight into the room past Ellory, who had been lingering outside the newly cleared doorway.

The room itself was square in shape, the parquet floor scratched and warped. A growth of vines stretched across the back wall, the leaves crushed and bleeding, forming a pool of shimmering gold on the floor.

Ellory stopped short.

"We need to leave. Now." He backed away from the pool, his whole body tensed.

"Why? What's wrong?"

Ellory grabbed her arm and dragged her back toward the door. He let go suddenly and began to pull at the door handle. It rattled and creaked, but would not budge. Ellory began to ramble as he tried to yank the door open.

"The vines, the gold pools - I knew this place was familiar. People started disappearing...They said it was some sort of chemical leak, I don't know. Look I'll tell you later, we have to get out of here first."

With that, the door handle came away from the door. Ellory stared down at it with a look of disbelief.

But her attention was on something altogether different. The figure was crouched right behind Ellory, a large crow bar clutched in one hand. Its head twisted slowly round, bringing an index finger up to where lips would have been. She tried to move towards it, but she was paralysed, watching as it giggled and brought the crowbar down on his back, before tackling him to the ground. It clawed and scratched and beat him with the bar, its manic laughter increasing the more he fought back. Finally, Ellory grabbed it by the waist and hurled it away from him.

Simultaneously, she felt herself being propelled back into the wall, a metal bar falling from her grasp. The icy numbness dissipated and she could finally move. Ellory was staring down at her, eyes wide in fear, pinning her arms to the floor. His face was scratched and bleeding, his hair matted with blood. She was completely disorientated, her head ringing and pain shooting across her back. She couldn't understand what Ellory was doing, why he was holding her down and not the girl.

Slowly, Ellory released his grip, taking the crowbar in his hand and rising to his feet. He backed away from her, holding the crowbar out toward her, making half-hearted jabs in the air. Realisation was only starting to hit her, her eyes welling up with tears. She reached out to him, and he paused for only a moment, before his demeanour hardened and he fled.

Ringing laughter and the patter of small footsteps reverberated around her, jeering and mocking. Her head seemed to tighten, and she felt as if she was deep underwater, the pressure increasing rapidly. The only thing she could think about were her hands, crimson, soaked in blood. Ellory's. The thought churned her stomach. She needed to get it off, to clean it, to scrub it from her skin. The pool caught her eye, and she crawled toward it.

Mesmerized, her fatigue and terror began to fade, as the magnetic attraction of the pool drew her forward. She cupped the iridescent liquid in her hands, cool to the touch. Before her eyes, the liquid darkened and began to seep into her skin, inky tendrils winding their way up her arm. The pain, initially only a slight tingling, increased exponentially. Vision deteriorating, she felt as if she was being frozen from the inside, the thudding of her slowing heartbeat blocking out every other noise. The floor gave way beneath her as she lost consciousness.

She awoke with a start. A sharp jolt of pain coursed through her body, jagged rock piercing her back. The air was stagnant and heavy, making it difficult to breathe. Her legs were enveloped in lengths of vine, and she clawed at them, releasing herself from their grip.

A blinking red light a few metres away caught her eye. She crawled forward, her muscles screaming as she inched toward it. Cold, sharp rock dug into her palms and tore at her knees. As she drew nearer, she could hear static - her radio.

With what remained of her energy, she tried to reach for it, but it slipped from her grip, the hard plastic clattering against the rock. The echoes grew fainter and fainter, before stopping with a muffled gurgle and splash.

Tumbling, limping, staggering, she rose to her feet and chased the sound. Drops of water dripped from the ceiling and trickled in miniature streams at her feet. The air grew thick with moisture and her progress slowed further; large crevices in the rock, covered over with thin layers of vines, were scattered throughout her path, and she fell many times, the wounds stinging with dirt and dust. All of a sudden the cavern seemed to open out and she could just make out a large expanse of water, murky and dark.

After a few moments, a faint red light flickered near the water's edge and she lurched forward, groping blindly in the water. The water was icy cold and the lakebed slimy, coils of vines entrenched in the rock. She grabbed the radio and switched on the attached flashlight, the pale blue beam barely illuminating a few metres around her.

Long objects seemed to float in the water, wrapped in a shroud of vines. She pointed the light toward them, counting around forty or so on the surface. She felt something brush against her ankles, and she shone the light down at her feet. A pale ashen hand twitched under the light. Startled, she sprang back, backing into the wall of the cave and straight into metal; a ladder.

She jumped and grasped the rung above her, her legs flailing trying to gain some purchase. The metal wheezed and creaked under the pressure as she clambered up, her feet slipping as the lower rungs began to crack and fall apart. A wooden board covered over the hole in the ceiling. She braced her shoulder against it and pushed herself up, the plank landing with a thud on the ground beside her.

A cloud of dust momentarily obscured her vision as she crawled out. The dust settled, and she found herself back in the main entrance hall, but this time it was dark; the musty smell of rotting wood and dust almost suffocating.

He was in the corner, his hands, stained with gold and blood, laying limp by his sides. She knelt beside him, and could see the ragged cuts, still slightly oozing red, all across his face. She could barely feel his pulse but he was still breathing. She managed to pull him to his feet, wrapping his arm around her shoulder and carrying him all the way out of the factory, beyond the fence and to the ship.

Scrambling up, she heaved him up onto the ship, the door whispering shut behind him. She slumped in her seat, starting up the engine in an exhausted daze. She set a course and then turned her attention to Ellory, who was still propped up against the wall where she left him, his skin changed to a worryingly bluish hue. She knelt beside him, shaking his arm, praying for him to be alright.

And that was how she was found hours later, barely conscious, softly begging for him to wake up.

But he never did.

The Man who lost his Spirit
Aaron Page

Once upon a time, there was a man who lived alone, within himself.

He had grown up in the city in a highrise block overlooking a bleak, disused car park where he played soccer with his friends most days. He was very shy as a teenager and believed he was worthless, talentless. He had lost his father when he was just seventeen and he harbored little hope that there would ever be anything else for him outside of his concrete jungle.

When he was eighteen he met a girl and fell in love. Suddenly his life was filled with colour and he glimpsed happiness for the very first time. He married and within two years, his wife had given birth to a daughter. He moved away with his family to a house near open fields, away from the city. Some years passed. Life was good. He was overjoyed when his wife told him the news that they were going to have another child.

But then, tragedy struck. The son that he had secretly wished for took a single breath at birth and was lost to them.

He held him only once, and then laid him under a row of large oak trees where he would remain in a sleep from which he could never wake.

They were heartbroken. Dark skies cloaked the graveyard as the wind shook the large oak trees violently above them. Everyone looked on in silence, their wishes and dreams buried beneath the cold clay.

On that day, the man lost something else. He did not know what it was, or even that he had lost it, but everyone else knew.

His wife knew.

His children knew.

His friends knew.

But he did not realise that on the day he had laid his son to rest, he had lost his spirit.

He worked at his job in an office and he got up at the same time each day. He came home at the same time each day. He had an ordinary life. He did his work and spoke very little to anyone. He had lost all interest in the sports he had loved and the music that he had once lived for.

There were people all around him who loved him and cared for him, but they were invisible to him.

***

Every day he would stare out at the cold, barren patch of land beside his house and wonder why he felt like this. All the invisible people around him would tell him things, but he could not hear them. The house of this man was cold and bare. The silence filled the whole day.

Christmas was no longer celebrated as it once was. The man just sat and watched television thinking of his lost boy, gone forever.

Then one day, his daughter had an idea to cheer him up. He should plant a tree for his lost son. The tree would grow tall and strong and he would plant it on the cold, barren patch of land beside his house where nothing had ever grown, only tall weeds and spiteful nettles.

***

He planted the tree, and then when he stared out at the cold, barren patch of land beside his house and wondered what was wrong, there was a tree before him, where once there had been nothing but tall weeds and spiteful nettles.

And then he had another idea. He would plant many things in the cold, barren patch of land beside his house, and it would not be so cold and barren anymore.

The man worked endlessly from one end of the day to the next. No word left his mouth but there was a hint of a smile on his face. His daughter could see a change in her father. So, one day she decided to help him. Slowly, without realising they started to form a bond.

***

Every day, he dug and toiled the land; he planted seeds and bulbs, flowers and shrubs, he watered his plants and watched them grow. He began to realise that the cold, barren patch of land beside his house was now a garden, and all the invisible people noticed that something about him had changed. They could not yet say what it was, but they just knew.

The man and his daughter sat outside in the garden drinking their cool drinks looking at the garden realising what they had achieved.

They looked at each other and smiled. He felt warm and happy again.

His wife looked out the window at her husband and daughter and silently wept as she saw this moment between them.

***

As the seasons passed, and the seasons turned into years, what was cold and barren before, became a place filled with colour and beauty. Every day, the moment he would awake, he would look out the window, and every day there was a new surprise that filled him with wonder and made him glad.

The bright sun of summer showed the beautiful colours of the garden. The glow that filled up the garden, amazed everyone that came to the house. The golden leaves in autumn and the snow that clung to the bare branches in winter slowly brought joy to the man's life. It helped him to live again and be part of his family. He had also formed a bond with his daughter and each day they would fix the garden, water the plants and take out the weeds.

***

Gradually he began to see his lost son's smile in the beauty of the flowers that blossomed in the summertime.

He listened to him laugh in the winds that stirred the shivering grasses.

He watched him play as the birds swooped and dived through the branches of the tree he had planted many years ago.

And the spirit he had lost a long time ago was found again, and the world was no longer invisible.

Forget Me, Forget Me Not
Diane Pasague

It is a warm day in autumn. The six o' clock sun is about to set and the withered leaves falling from the oak trees lessen as the evening wind moves far away.

At the corner of the meadow, the oldest oak tree in the wood stands with its century old branches accommodating the different colours of the Fall. Two small figures emerge from the stoned path that trails the side of the gigantic tree.

The slightly larger of the two runs messily to a pile of fallen leaves that had built up into a small mountain. He kicks his legs around until they rain heavily on top of him. The boy raises his arms and jogs in circles, attempting to savor the moment.

The smaller of the two can only stare with suppressed amusement, amazed and in awe of her older friend. When most of the leaves have fallen, the girl laughs out loud, feeling the thrill of the boy's actions.

"C'mon! It's your turn!" the boy urges.

The girl grins widely, eyes sparkling as she revels in the boy's attention. She runs, copying his movements. Although she is slightly slower, her small feet are still able to lift just as many leaves off the pavement.

The chaotic rustling of the wind and trees settle and the two companions smile at each other, sharing the unspoken benevolence in the air.

-Present Day-

Waking up like he just slept in Satan's lair wasn't exactly how Nate wanted to spend this particular morning. He can feel sticky wet hair stuck to his forehead as he struggles to move his limbs. His eyelids only open to thin slits. Realising his situation, Nate groans inwardly. He waits a few seconds before willing his arm to reach for his cell phone.

The screen flares violently not even a second after Nate turns on his phone. His dry eyes scrunch up painfully in protest.

Again, he waits until his senses come back. But, his alertness comes whirling out of nowhere once he focuses on the notification that seems to scream at him.

23 Missed Calls

11 New Messages

Shit.

Nate lazily dumps the phone beside his pillow and rubs his fingertips hard against his eyes, leaving damp palms pressing against his face. The thought of going to work doesn't even deserve last place on his to-do list this morning.

Unpredictably, getting up is not the hardest part. No. It's stripping down naked in a freezing bathroom and then taking a shower in water that is equally cold.

Nate mentally applauds himself because last night, in his not-so-sober state, he had forgotten to turn on the heating for the next day. Not to mention that shortly after getting dressed, there is a small visit from the old lady in the next apartment who rants about her six year old granddaughter hearing a stream of profanities from the open balcony.

Fortunately, she embarks on a profound lecture about keeping 'a certain standard' for the level of innocence in today's youth and questions how a grown man such as Nate could live with himself after displaying such 'bitter negativity'.

However, Nate can't register anything she is saying. Instead he chooses to focus on two white hairs that protude from a large wart at the corner of her bottom lip and wonders if it ever felt tickly whenever she spoke. He winces at that last thought.

***

The grass feels unusually warm. Just in the distance where the tops of the trees meet the old sky, one could witness a deep orange and fuchsia colliding on a blue canvas.

The two lie completely flat on the grass, staying close enough that their hands would brush off one another from every small movement. Though each time they do, the little girl feels an irrepressible spark that rushes through her arm. A quiet agreement leaves a comforting silence hanging between the two friends.

Two pairs of eyes stare blankly up at the now amber sky, absentmindedly following the slow wispy clouds or the occasional lone bird that floats by.

"Nate" the girl breathes.

The boy hums in response, eyes slowly closing. The girl turns her head to glance at her friend.

"What're we doing here?" she says with a small voice.

The corners of the boy's lips quirk up slightly, "I dunno", he responds simply. The girl watches as his dazed eyes gaze in her direction.

"I just like it here."

The latter stares for a second, mesmerised by the surprising seriousness she sees on the boy's face. However, the brief look in his eyes doesn't go unnoticed before she splutters out her next words, unconvincingly hiding a flushed face.

"Cos there aren't any grown-ups here?"

The boy chews on his bottom lip and squints his eyes as if trying to look at something distant. He seems to contemplate for a while until the little girl sees his eyes widen again, lips pursed.

"Yeah…" Nate exasperates. He smiles idiotically when the girl bursts out laughing in a squeaky voice, which eventually dies down into small fits of giggles.

"You know, if you don't like it here, then you don't have to come with me every time", the boy states matter-of-factly.

The girl's eyes grow bigger when she realises what she has implied.

"NO! No! I-," a slight wave of panic runs through her head, "I just wan'ed to know, uhm, why you... like it here so much."

She looks at her friend nervously, watching his eyebrows un-knot. His lips straighten into a line, followed by prolonged 'oh'.

The boy fiddles with the hem of his shirt, contemplating his answer. He goes back to staring up at the darkening sky. The girl does the same, although subtly hesitating as she eyes the boy curiously.

***

After an undeniably life-changing cup of coffee and a phone call to a very reluctant co-worker, Nate is almost capable of functioning like a human being whilst succeeding in calling in sick for the day.

Although a few hours of TV and a bowl of cereal later, he realizes that he still had planned to go somewhere after work today.

Nate makes sure he is wrapped up in all kinds of thick clothing before stepping out from the lobby and onto a busy sidewalk. He has a somewhat 'date' prepared for the afternoon.

***

Nate had already thought about exactly why he liked it here. Why it meant anything to him. 'Why' it was the only place in their town that he could run away to and hide safely away with his own imagination.

He eventually learned why it was the one place where no grown-up could tear this imagination down or no bulky sixth grader could steal it from him. He knows for certain now.

This place was drastically lonely, but in its own way, it was enchanting. The tall, mysterious trees that hid years of secret memories and their leaves that always danced with the wind, the scent of the earth and cleansed air, the small woodland animals chatting in the background and the way the late sun would shine so brightly on the meadow right before it retired for the day - all of it - was what made this place so separated from everything else.

The girl looks at their surroundings from where she lies as a lopsided smile plays on Nate's lips.

***

He only has to walk a few blocks before he stops in front of a small and quaint flower boutique. At this time, only a few people are inside the pastel-coloured shop. A sophisticated-looking, middle aged lady walks slowly past the display of tulips at one corner of the shop while two adolescent girls wearing schools uniforms debate over the display of roses at the front of the store.

Nate walks timidly through the entrance, feeling a bit out of place. The shop clerk, a frail woman who looks like she was near the age of forty, approaches him.

"Can I help you, Sir?" she asks, bearing a small smile. He pauses momentarily before realising he has no idea what he wanted to buy.

"Er, yes, please."

"Are you buying flowers for your wife?" the lady asks, a polite tone hanging to her voice. Nate has to chuckle at her question. He replies in an amused tone, "No, no ma'am." He grins sheepishly while holding up both hands to show that they are bare. "It's for a person that's very special to me. I'm seeing her today actually, around an hour from now, so..."

The lady gives him a look before laughing briefly at his words. She lightly sets a slender finger on her lips whilst thinking. She directs Nate to the farthest end of the shop. Stopping abruptly at a small section on the wall, the lady points behind the glass that contains a row of flowers, all different in type and colour but every single one looked vibrantly pleasant. However, the small bunch of flowers gathered at the left-hand side was what immediately caught Nate's attention.

The flowers look similar to daisies but instead of a snowy white, the petals are blue. The kind of blue found in an evening sky, right before sunset. They look simple. But to Nate, his thoughts direct towards a certain somebody. They remind him of a familiar innocence and a pretty face that feels so vague in his mind.

The shop clerk follows his eyes, slightly surprised by his sudden change in expression. Her face wanders in the direction Nate is staring. Then, almost as if she can effortlessly read his mind, she decides to speak up first.

"They're called Forget-Me-Nots."

***

"You don't have to understand, at least you came here with me," Nate says. And almost like a whisper, he continues softly, "Thanks."

His friend doesn't have to wonder why he has said it so sincerely. Nate knows how much she has risked just by taking a step out of her house. Almost every night he would hear her. He would hear the loud screaming and shouting from her house next door, way past midnight. The violent and slurred words her mother would spit out at her when she'd had just a little too much sometimes. He would flinch at the sound of hard objects striking already-bruised skin. Nate had always been awake, listening to the girl's raw screams and held back sobs.

When he was sure her mother had finally locked her in the bedroom, he would climb out of his bed and sit against the wall under his window. Every night he would stay there, waiting until the crying and hiccups stopped, listening closely until the girl cried herself to sleep. Only then could Nate properly find a way to close his eyes and relax.

"S'okay, I don't think my Mom's gonna be home 'til later anyway," she responds reassuringly. Nate tries hard to ignore the worry in her voice.

***

It's sunset. The sound of the city traffic becomes quieter as Nate walks further into the sea of dark green and grey. The gravel pavement leads him to an almost empty area near two, very large cherry blossom trees that overlook a wide plain of freshly cut grass.

Whilst walking down the last aisle towards the mass of pink and white flowers, Nate glances respectfully at the grey stones that vary in size and shade, each lining up beside the pathway. A few look very old and dusty. Others still have long-dead, withered flowers at the bottom with only a few bearing fresh ones at their feet. He thinks back to the conversation with the lady from the flower shop.

"I think I've heard that name before."

"A lot of people know the name but never really know what they look like," she replied. The lady stared sympathetically at the small flowers.

"You know, Forget-Me-Nots are pretty much self-explanatory. In life, they symbolise a promise of never forgetting someone important that you've lost in the past."

***

"But you know I'll always be wherever you are, right?" the girl says brightly. And Nate can't help but gawk at her sudden confidence. Immediately, a playful smirk finds its way on Nate's face.

"Stalker!" he blurts out teasingly.

The girl feigns a hurt expression before her mouth twists funnily, failing to keep an almost successful poker face when Nate throws his head back, laughing.

***

Kneeling carefully on the grass, Nate fluidly places the Forget-Me-Nots right under the golden engraved words on the tombstone. He sits back on his knees and reads the name on the dark marble.

Nate had forgotten how many times he'd seen and read those words. He reads the name again, lightly brushing his fingertips along the outline of each letter. He sees light pink petals slowly moving with the wind, making their way across the ground. Some petals stick on to the ends of Nate's coat.

His eyes shut firmly. And Nate finds he wants to remember her face again.

"The sun's about to set," the girl says.

"We should probably go then," he says, *"ready?"*

"I'm ready when you are".

Plan D
Ghail Protacio

It's almost amusing how some people make such a big deal out of last days. On the last day of elementary school everybody hugged each other and cried and drenched each other's shoulders with their try-hard tears as if they weren't going to have any form of communication at all in the next few days. And there I was rolling my eyes in the corner and making plans with Peter (codename: Spidey) for that following summer. The last day my brother spent in hospital after breaking his arm, we went out to dinner as a family – minus Dad – to celebrate. And the very last day the biological father stayed with us before he left, Mom cried, and Brother-of-the-Year Lucas taught me how to leave a dent the exact size and shape of my fist in the deadbeat's car.

Despite it all, truth is, nobody's going to be there to tell you about all the last days you're going to have in this life, and there's a lot as it is already. Where was my cake on the day I finally stopped bothering to dot my I's with my trademark skull and crossbones? Who was there to mourn my favourite pair of jeans' last day of being wearable? See, everybody misses all of these other last days and I don't see any of them crying too hard about it. So, why should my last day living be any different?

Today, I took the responsibility upon myself to remind Mom not to cry when I die. I'd told her countless times before already so it wouldn't seem too out of the blue when the day finally came. I felt like I could've picked a better time to tell her today though, rather than in the middle of dinner preparation because the next thing I know – she starts pointing a very large knife dangerously close to my face.

"Ron Edward Porter, I swear to God you will outlive your own mother."

The sharp steel point of the knife threatened the existence of my nose as it glinted in Colorado's 5 o'clock sunlight. It peered in through a trio of open windows behind Mom, the weakness of its heat reminding us summer's goodbyes were due. I kind of half-wished that she stab me right then and there, but then I thought that there were way cooler and prouder ways to die than taking a knife to the face from the woman who gave you life in the first place.

"I mean, you know I'm getting old, Red. Lucas already left us for college and it won't be long 'til you're gone too. You're graduating this year, for crying out loud! And you'll both probably be too busy with your own families to notice when I die alone on a random day, but just know that I –"

I'd heard it all before, so I didn't consider it rude to walk out before she could finish.

Mom had this problem of thinking too far ahead into the future. That was basically all she knew – it was too painful for her to even take a glimpse into the past and there wasn't anything she was that grateful for in the present. So she hoped and doubted about changes that hadn't happened yet. I, on the other hand, could've passed for the opposite. Every time they used to get us to imagine ourselves in 'ten years from now' in school, I'd see nothing. My mind would go blank, and I couldn't even imagine what job I'd have, if any, if I'd have my own place, if Mom would be there or if I'd live the life of a complete loner sheltered from the rest of existence. I saw myself watching reruns of yesterday's cartoons, if that counted. But otherwise I had no goals, no ambitions, and that was all I knew. I mean, I just turned eighteen last month, and I was already done with being eighteen.

I dragged my footsteps down the hall into my room. The door was heavy and closed with a loud thud behind me, and I'm not going to lie, I jumped a little no matter how many times it had happened before. Back then when Lucas was still around he'd lend me his skateboard and leave it leaning against my door to hold it open. He spent a good part of his life in the room opposite me but he'd do the same to his own door with his scooter, and we would acknowledge this open-door brother code that we never really gave an official meaning to. But the last time that happened was already a little over a year ago, and so vanished the reason for open doors and secret codes, other than my last text to Spidey, which read: 22:21. Be ready.

It's funny how even just weeks ago, we would've taken 'Be ready' as something along the lines of 'Dude, make sure you have some pants on by the time we get there,' or vice versa. But now somehow we'd switched the meaning to subtly saying our goodbyes for the last time.

My own suicide letter was sitting patiently on my desk. It was a crisp white envelope sitting atop graffiti names (mostly repeated scribbles of 'SPIDEY WUZZ HERE') scrawled on dirty wood. I didn't get to write it until the night before. It must've escaped my mind that I had to write one, along with the thought that someone could even care that I was gone.

But all in all, I was quite proud of my work. I managed to combine eighteen different ways of saying goodbye – a combination of different expressions and languages alike. Mom had this collection of dictionaries of languages she wished she took up but didn't, which proved useful for me during my lack of inspiration at three in the morning. She'd know it was me once she read the opening:

Dear Mom, what's 'red', pale-skinned and possibly even more pale-skinned or decaying by the time you're reading this? Adios.

I was cynical when I felt like it. I knew I was planning to break the news too harshly for my mother but knowing her, one day, regardless of how many years it'd take, she'd look back on all of this and laugh. And I was counting on that one laugh to free me of guilt in the afterlife.

***

I didn't remember falling asleep but somehow, I ended up having to drag myself to a state of consciousness. Forcing my eyes open revealed that I had made a soft landing on my bed during the act of passing-out that I couldn't even recall. A mess of two pillows and an unmade duvet cover cushioned my face, the light blue fabric stained navy from involuntary drool. I pried myself off of the bed and sat up. My hands were gripping the edge of my mattress to take a moment to come back to the world. It took me a while to notice the screen of black invading my window, as well as the fact that I had somewhere to be. So clumsily, I fished for my phone in the sky-coloured sea of my bed covers.

9:36pm. Not bad. I mentally congratulated myself for not waking up tragically later. I mean, how weird would it be to be labelled as the guy who showed up late to his own planned death? But in order to avoid ending up as that guy, I had to bolt out of there, fast.

Of course, Mom stopped me in the hallway, curious as to why her son was sporting the latest style in Homeless-Man fashion while rushing out the door. I don't even think I remembered to put shoes on. So, as usual, she convinced me to have dinner first, and after gulping down a whole portion of chicken and vegetables, some water, with a side of hiccups, I thought I was free to go. I was wrong.

9:49pm and Mom asked where I was heading.

"Out," I said.

"Where out?"

"A party," I lied.

"Dressed like that?"

"Well, of course I plan to put shoes on, Mom."

"Go get dressed, Red. I don't want Mrs. Wilson next door to be bugging me about not buying my children decent clothes. You have nice clothes, go wear them."

"What am I supposed to wear?" Having no recollection of the contents of my wardrobe, I blinked at her.

"How about your Church clothes?"

I didn't go to Church anymore, but I vaguely remembered a light gray polo shirt and slacks stuffed in the back of my closet.

"Fine." I started walking back towards my room.

"Oh, and wear those dress shoes I got you last Christmas!" Mom yelled behind me.

I paused.

"The what?"

"The dress shoes."

"...Are they black and fancy?"

"Yes, Red."

"Got it."

***

And so explains how I ended up running for my life at around 10:13pm in order to be punctual for my death. The place we agreed to meet was about a ten minute walk from my house, hopefully half the time if I ran. I planned to take my time beforehand and pick out all the things I wouldn't miss in this town but everything around me quickly became no more than racing pictures as I wore out the soles of the dress shoes. Not to mention it was dark and getting significantly colder out, the only possible solution of keeping warm being to keep running. I was already losing my breath when a glimpse of a swing set caught my eye. I mentally crossed the neighbourhood playground off my list. I was done with that place ever since Bruce Talston repeatedly pulled down my pants every time he caught my legs on the swing when I was six.

By 10:20pm, in record-breaking time, I arrived at the destination in a sweaty, panting mess. Spidey picked out the place. It was an old corner store that shut down months ago when the owner went bankrupt. His uncle was planning to buy the property and, being broke and desperate, the owner let Spidey use the place for a few hours or so to check it out and send good word to his uncle. Highly doubtful.

The place was small but big enough to fit us all. I stumbled in through the back door to find the other guys sitting cross-legged in a circle on the ground. Almost all of them were dressed in hoodies, tshirts and jeans. I went over to join them awkwardly, filling in the space between Colin Halsey and Brook Keller.

"Nice outfit, Ron Edward. When's the funeral?"

Spidey's face appeared opposite me. A smirk was slowly growing on his lips underneath where his mark of masculinity should have been. Unfortunately ridiculously baby-faced, an insult from Spidey never did break me.

"Mine or yours?"

A mixture of dry laughs acknowledged my reply while Spidey faked applause.

"Touché, Ron Edward. Now, let's get started. It is now thirty seconds past 22:21 and now my good friend, Ron Edward has kindly joined us. I didn't wanna have to go all 'Mr. Park' on you guys, but I gotta see who's here. Roll call!"

'Mr. Park' was Spidey's mature, obsessively-organised, teacher-like alter ego. It was funny because his amazingly youthful looks said otherwise, especially when both traits were put together. The guy was eighteen but could leave you wondering whether he was twelve or thirty five at any one time.

Spidey cleared his throat.

"First of all, Miss Cynthia Mae Dayton?"

"Present."

All eyes turned to the small blonde sitting two spaces away from Spidey's left. I didn't recall seeing her before. I didn't even remember her being at any of the other meetings before tonight, but I found myself mumbling too easily.

"May Day…"

Her eyes glanced up at me from across the room and I had to scoot back a little from her deep brown stare. It was as if I had unintentionally revealed a dark secret of hers, or maybe even something along the lines of an online videogame username. She definitely came across as the 'shut-in-gamer' type to me. The awkwardness left us a minute of silence before Spidey decided to clear the air and continue.

"Colin Halsey?"

Colin, on my right said, "Yup."

"Seth Jameson?"

"Here."

"Brook Keller?"

"Yessir."

"Dexter Keller?"

"Uh huh."

Brook's routine of severe eye-rolling and scoffing at her younger brother was too obvious to go unnoticed. He seemed to follow everything she did, even in her escape to get away from her life of being followed.

"Peter Park, oh yes, I'm here." Spidey paused before getting to me. "And last but not least, we are all aware of the presence of dear old Ron Edward here."

I only nodded.

"Okay, that's all of us. By the way, guys, Cynthia Mae over here will be joining us for the first and last time tonight, in case none of you noticed she was new."

I noticed. May Day raised her hand slightly, but she didn't wave.

Spidey spent the next fifteen minutes asking us whether we were prepared for what was going to happen, making sure our suicide notes were in check and all that. Then he went ahead to explain to us (again) just how things were going to work. We were far from professionals. Granted, we were seven kids in high school who accidentally met and realized we all just wanted to end it for good. We had no access to drugs and none of us were patient enough to wait for pills to kill us. We had one gun courtesy of Spidey's connections. Seven bullets. Five minutes more or less. Less.

We agreed that Seth Jameson would go first, after coming to the conclusion that the most desperate should get the first opportunity. He'd be shot by Colin, and then the gun would fall into the hands of Brook who'd help Colin kill himself. The task of killing Brook would go to Dexter (she said she didn't mind who shot her as long as she died before her brother), Dexter to Spidey, Spidey to me, and the pleasure of killing yours truly would go to May Day. They all suggested she was the bravest based on rumours that seemed to have somehow missed me. But after that, she would turn the gun on herself, pull the trigger and none of us would ever know what happened next.

Seth stepped up while Spidey took out the gun from his backpack and handed it to Colin. Colin positioned the weapon hesitantly. He didn't seem sure of where to put it.

"Head's fine, bro," Seth assured him, waiting. The gun was gently being pushed against his temple.

"Okay," Spidey interrupted. "Ready, get Seth…"

He meant to pause for us to acknowledge his misplaced pun but before Colin could cock the gun and Spidey finish his sentence, we heard the sound of footsteps. Footsteps outside of the seven pairs of planted feet in the space we occupied. An intruder's footsteps.

***

We froze. Colin pulled the gun to his side and I listed a whole group of possible suspects for the owner of the mystery feet off of the top of my head. Mom followed me – that was my top suspicion. Mr. Gutierrez, the butcher a block away, grew suspicious of the number of teenagers heading in this direction and called the cops on us to check. A local passing by decided to be more adventurous. Whoever it was, we were about to find out.

Our guest showed up clad in black, gloves, ski mask and all.

"Oh," I said, slightly relieved to see him instead of my mother. But then I found myself the target of wide-eyed stares and it wasn't until I noticed the gun pointed at me that I found out why. "OH."

"Dammit, Red, run!"

I ducked, missing the complementary advice from a distressed Seth, and heard a gunshot behind me.

"Everybody get down!"

We all obeyed Mr. Pushy and put our hands on our heads before he could suggest that too.

"Throw your wallets over here."

He strode over to Brook, violently pulling her up as she tried to keep from squealing. He slid an arm under her throat and threatened her at gunpoint while piles of wallets fell at his feet. Brook squirmed as the grip tightened. It was suddenly harder to breathe, not just for her but for the rest of us too.

"All of you!"

He glared at me yet again. Half-shaking, I reached into my pocket and tossed him mine. He tugged the damsel in distress down along with him as he bent down to pick up my faded khaki wallet alone out of the others. We waited, without any of us uttering even a syllable, as the thief ripped my wallet open, wincing as the Velcro scratched at our ears. He paused, and although we couldn't see his face all that well, I could already tell I'd woken an already-alert beast.

"What the hell is this?!" He seemed to roar at us, as such a creature does, and waved my last good buck too close to Brook's face.

"Umm…" I hesitated at first.

So Spidey covered for me.

"That, Mister, is a one dollar bill."

That didn't help at all. If anything, it only encouraged his anger. Our visitor could have breathed out fire with the look he shot at us. He seemed to know he intimidated us and used that to his advantage by pointing his gun up at the ceiling, not even counting down as he pulled the trigger.

"Christ! Okay! Okay!" Spidey fell down to his knees with the rest of us.

The explosive ricochet of the bullet convinced us all to cover our ears and drive ourselves into reciting strings and strings of silent prayers, regardless of whether or not any of us were religious. The only other choice was to shut our eyes and pretend we weren't there.

***

I was at home. With Mom. Lucas came to visit. He brought a friend from college. We were all going to have chicken and vegetables for dinner. That delicious grilled chicken Mom learned how to make from that one celebrity cooking show.

Everything was going well until I heard another shot fire.

Oh, God. Brook wasn't dead. She was alive and breathing. She came to join us for dinner too. She sat down opposite me and complimented the chicken. I told her Mom made it. Mom smiled at her.

Dexter's voice rang out a scream, and then another bullet was shot.

Mom answered the door. It was Dexter. He was looking for Brook. Mom said he might as well stay for dinner too so he sat down beside his sister. She rolled her eyes again.

Another shot.

Mom had to pull out a stool to make room for Seth to sit at our dining table. She fixed him up his own plate and told him to sit down. He liked the chicken too.

Another.

We were done with dinner. Colin came over and we all went to watch TV in the living room.

Another.

I introduced Mom to May Day. She came to visit us and brought videogames. I was right about her being the videogame type. We all took turns playing.

Another. Tears were threatening to roll down my cheek at this stage.

Spidey showed up. He broke May Day's high score for killing the most zombies. She challenged him to a one-on-one game and reclaimed her title.

I was waiting for it. The last bullet that would kill me. I was shaking. I had to hug my knees so tightly because I was that afraid of slipping away too easily. I was scared. I didn't want to go anymore. What would happen to Mom? To Lucas? To Brook, and Dexter, and Seth, and Colin, and May Day and Spidey's parents, and family, and relatives, and distant relatives, and friends, and friends of friends, and acquaintances, and classmates and anyone else they'd ever spoken to in their lives? I didn't want to be a link in this messed-up chain of tragedies anymore. I didn't want the last conversation I had with Mom to be about clothes I was going to die in. I didn't want to be a name listed in next week's obituary anymore. I wanted out. Dear God, I wanted out.

***

A gun cocked.

"Red." Spidey's voice.

"Red." May Day's voice.

"Red." Brook, Dexter, Seth and Colin's.

I froze as I was. I had to be imagining things again. The dinner, the chicken, the video games – I was on the road to going insane and I knew it.

"Dammit, Red!" Spidey again.

I meant to ignore it, but being roughly pushed to the ground stopped me. I opened my eyes. Spidey, Brook, Dexter, Colin, Seth and May Day – all in one piece. Each, I mean.

"Now that you're done avoiding things, we thought you'd want us to let you know what went down."

I shifted my eyes across the room and found the thief lying on the floor to my left. He was still breathing, clutching onto a wound on his thigh. He glowered at me, but I turned my attention back to the others too quickly to notice any more unfriendly gestures.

"Colin shot him. But he missed the first time," Spidey paused to glare at Colin. "Luckily for him, he accidentally shot the gun out of Mr. Gimme-Your-Wallet's hand. Then he almost hit Dexter."

"Oops."

"Then Seth."

"Sorry about that."

"Then almost shot at his foot."

"Guilty."

"Then just barely missed Cynthia Mae."

"Again, sorry."

"And then finally, he succeeded."

I was still in shock and at a loss for words, even though truthfully, Brook should've been the one in my place, me just being the guy who thought all his fellow suicide companions were dead.

"There's one bullet left though. Wanna do the honours and shoot it at something?" I nodded to accept Colin's offer and got up to take the gun from his hands.

The last bullet. The one that should've killed May Day, and then would've killed me. The thought mesmerized me. In my trance I ended up twirling the deadly contraption around in my fingers to play with the curve of the trigger. I aimed, tilting it upwards before holding my breath and firing blindly as the seventh bullet shot up to the ceiling.

The police siren's song playing in the distance meant about as much to us as the music that plays at the end credits of a movie.

A Poetic Fix

Maeve Sweeney

I have a serious and passionate hatred towards the subject of mathematics. Mainly due to the fact that this disaster all centres around the original, catastrophic equation. An equation that caused me a broken heart and two solid months of detention.

Take a father, a typical Irish father. A man with the ability to complain endlessly about the state of the Irish economy, to whom swearing comes as naturally as converting oxygen to carbon dioxide and who amazingly always has a fascinating story from his youth to dazzle us with after having one too many in the local.

Add a mother, a not so typical Irish mother, a woman with exotic, radiant looks. Looks that force you to assume she has just landed on this god-forsaken, rain-infested island. However upon her opening her mouth and greeting you with a mere 'Hello' the accent that emanates in so flat and intimidatingly Dublin that any idea of foreign origin is washed away in a nano-second. I have it on good authority that she has never fully pronounced a word ending in 'T' in her life and family legend states that her first words ever spoken were 'feck off'.

Throw in a equals sign and the result is me. Now, there is a serious reason why I never mentioned my Father's looks and Mother's personality. Growing up people expected me to be loud, confident, good-humoured, witty and breathtakingly beautiful. I, however, am irritatingly awkward, not the average textbook's definition of attractive, I may have the temper of a hormonal bull trapped in a scarlet room and am about as witty as a punctured tennis ball. Bear all this in mind as I bestow upon you my tale, I cannot be held wholly responsible for my actions. The maths is at fault.

A good fairytale usually starts with a 'Once Upon A Time', yet I consider myself far too modern and mature to dally in things like 'Once Upon A Time's. So I shall begin my story with the far more appropriate; it started with a conversation with myself. I am always baffled when people say that they do not talk to themselves. Are you all stupid? Who will ever know you as well, understand your humour, appreciate your opinion and accept your pre-existing little quirks and flaws as much as you, yourself will? People can you not see that you are the best company that you could ever wish for?

So there I was arguing with myself over whether I should have the chicken or curry noodles for lunch, a vital decision in any young lady's life, when I saw him slowly shuffle past my kitchen window. I swear to you the breath was knocked out of me. To this day Eamon argues-

Oh right, Eamon. My apologies, I seem to have forgotten the living specimen that is my brother Eamon. To sum him up in few words is difficult. He has the looks, the personality and a willingness to embrace life without hesitation. It is a true shame that he is never sober enough to enjoy it. I still regarded him with nothing short of adoration, oblivious to his weakness for anything with a price and a promise of a buzz. I looked upon Eamon as if he were the Messiah and I the devoted follower. Though I never really heard him say anything, bar the string of constant muttered 'Jesus, Mary and Josephs' that I was graced with whenever in his company. Basically Eamon is the perfect combination of Father and Mother. That equation had a result beyond comparison.

Anyway - To this day Eamon argues that I could not breathe due to the puffs of black smoke which were flowing freely from the pot of my now cremated noodles, but to nobody's sincere surprise he was, is wrong. That boy stole my heart and my ability to consume oxygen in one moment of pure brilliance.

They call it love at first sight, just don't ask me who 'they' are, and it truly was love. A love that changed everything. I finally got the point of all those romantic comedies I was forced to endure during endless sleepovers at my friend's houses, finally understood the sappy lyrics of

80's love ballads, finally saw what Shakespeare was ranting on about in 'Shall I Compare Thee'. Shakespeare you were some man, I hope you got her in the end (or him, my apologies Shakespeare). It was that very moment that it all clicked and the suppressed, creative valve in my body burst releasing the immediate, heavy flow of all things beautiful and imaginative. I was hooked, drawn to this stranger like a junkie to their fix. I forgot all reason, all knowledge of how one 'should' act, all cautionary tales I was told during youth and, quite frankly, the meaning of the word subtle. And was overcome with a passion so intense that I blurted out the lines that started it all.

'You were sent from up above

To sprinkle my existence with love

My heart you did play

As you stole it away

On the crystal white wings of a dove'

Following this minor creative outburst I went to seek the advice of the only one capable of advising me, I went to have my fourth ever conversation with my brother. the first three mainly consisting of him scolding me and a use of innuendo I was far too young to comprehend. He was in his room, a room I had always feared entering. I, once again, could not breathe. This time it was due to the revolting stench that hung over all his possessions, the pong of old tobacco, unwashed clothes and also a smell my youthful nostrils were not yet accustomed to. I blinked away the tears the stink brought to my eyes and saw Eam asleep on a pile of clothes that belonged in some highly-quarantined area. His mouth hung open in the most attractive way, a milky white string of drool flowing from him mouth and onto the sleeve of his leather jacket.

I contemplated pouring a bucket of cold water over his head, but quickly dismissed the idea, knowing full well that the heroine of a love story would never even dream of doing something so drastic. I settled for shaking his shoulder vigorously until he showed clear signs of consciousness.

"So, if you wanted to catch a boys attention what would you do?" Abrupt I admit but I believe the general point was well made.

"Are you implyin' my interest in boys or yours, baby sis?" was his garbled response, so perhaps the first point was not as well made as originally thought.

"Be serious Eam, for God's sake, we all know your string of suitors has never featured a male. that homophobic cow, what's her name?, Ma's Aunt Lucy will be singing in her grave."

"Right, now that we know Aunt Lucy is singing my praises from beyond the grave, would you like to tell me who in the are you talkin' about?"

"Excuse me!" I spluttered "He is my William Darcy, my Romeo Montague, my Heathcliff, hell, he is my Edward Cullen."

My efforts were met with an amused smile, positively dripping in sarcasm. He still shockingly had the decency to reply.

"And, will I be fortunate enough to get a description? Oh no, let me guess. He is a classically handsome, honourable man of society, no?, a hot-headed, love-obsessed teenager. Nope, that is you. A wild tortured soul, handsome and rugged, ah Jesus, just don't tell me he sparkles."

"Don't be a complete eejit Eam, he obviously doesn't sparkle. He does, however, have hair as golden and luscious as a Crunchie, eyes that could turn metamorphic rock into diamonds with one smouldering glance and skin as smooth and faultless as an egg, though with much less visible pores."

"Well now, Crunchies and eggs, I don't believe you can get more romantic than that." He said in one of the most patronising tones I have ever heard. "I do believe you are talking about Shane O'Malley, he moved down on Sherbert's Row there a few weeks back. His Da drives one of those big, fancy Jeepy yokes. I say they're absolutely minted. Go on, little sis, marry the son and we'll be loaded."

I did not hear half of what Eamon said as my life had just taken on a whole new meaning. Shane O'Malley. Shane, no word could ever be as beautiful as his name, no combination of vowels and consonants could ever have the effect that those five letters had on me,no name would ever make me feel so alive and, admittedly, nervous as the perfect Shane, Shane O'Malley. I was inspired to compose yet another love poem in honour of the milestone that was finding out his name.

'My life, my Shane O'Malley

Let us be, there is no time to dally

If my life was a play

Depicting each day

Your arrival will be the finale'

Not my best work but one must get over these things. I was given some interesting advice following the most recent lapse in concentration, resulting in that poetic masterpiece and was soon on my way to making poor Shane O'Malley fall in love with me.

I would find deep pleasure in telling you that over those following weeks myself and Eamon bonded in a way that most siblings do during the very early years of childhood. That is simply not the case. To me he was my partner in crime, the genius behind the epic plan, the one who would help me land Shane O'Malley and whose brotherly instincts had just taken slightly longer to develop. Alas, to him I was a mere plaything, a form of entertainment, who was fun to mess with and watch ruin their life. He was the cruel child with the magnifying glass burning the ant, and I the helpless ant running pointlessly around trying to escape the impending doom. If only I had known Eam's true intentions, I may have been saved the heartbreak of a thousand scorned lovers, abandoned by their betrothed.

It took me almost three weeks to get everything together and ready, Eamon had said that it was vital that I did it publicly. He was an expert on the confusing topic that was teenage love. Those three weeks were the most nerve-wracking yet exhilarating weeks of my life. Torn between my love for O'Malley and my fear of being a social outcast, I chose the former, naturally.

He was just so beautiful, in a manly way of course. To be perfectly honest I'm not sure you could him intelligent exactly, but, he certainly had a unique mental wave pattern and I believe that counts for something. My school life thrived of the hope that a teacher would ask him a question and I would once again hear him yawn and mumble "Uh, How'm I, like, supposed to know, you know!" Oh, I loved how he said that, always those exact words, so simple yet so powerful, sort of.

Yes that whole 'like' thing irritated me after a while, it wasn't that he said 'like' or even the way he said 'like'. I was annoyed that everyone else started to use it just because he did. I'm sure that before O'Malley's arrival there was an occasional slip of the tongue where the accidental 'like' slipped out, but, once my O'Malley began to use 'like' it was like an out-break of Swine Flu or Ringworm. It was ridiculous! I could not walk five steps without hearing that stupid word, and at one point got so frustrated by my sheep-like peers that it all became too much and I exploded with the following. A poem, you may be shocked to discover, which somehow in all my exasperation still related back to O'Malley's beauty.

'Wow, can you see that moon?

Beautiful as any, like, tune

So pretty and round

I am, like, spellbound

And this moment a sun would just ruin, like'

But then it was just unbearable. Coming out of O'Malley's mouth the word seemed mysterious yet somehow still safe, confident yet reserved. On the other hand 'like' coming out of everyone elses' mouths just sounded like an irritating, single-syllabled noise that was said with little individuality and practically no conviction.

I rose early on the twenty-fifth of March, spirits high and heart-rate rocketing. For some reason I was able to ignore the horrific plague that was the jitters, anyway Eamon had assured me with the utmost sincerity that our plan would be a success. Up until this point my little hints and subtle nudges had gone unnoticed, what I mean by that was Shane O'Malley had not yet fallen in love with me. I skipped into the kitchen, light as air, on love's wings, remembering the first time he had looked at me. As one might imagine I came up with a few lines of nonsensical verse to celebrate the occasion, but this milestone was too humongous for me to merely recite my poetry to myself. Perhaps coming across as a bit crazy. I went a step further, I wrote it down on a piece of thick, heavily fragranced parchment and put it in his school locker. I don't know if he ever got the full effect of the rose scented pages as his locker absolutely stank of Lynx Apollo. However, no amount of mose poisoning, throat closing aerosol could take away the meaning of those carefully composed words.

'Oh, on this day I know that you saw me

I know, how simply great can our lives be?

From dusk until dawn

Our love carries on

You would have to be blind to not see'

Eamon was sitting at the kitchen table, rather noisily devouring a cinnamon bagel and coffee. I glided past him dropping him a less than subtle wink. I was in such a cheeky mood, knowing that today was the day that I was going to tell both O'Malley and indeed the rest of the World the sheer depth of my love. And so my day began…..

I arrived in school in the best of spirits, I was young, optimistic, naive and completely smitten. The morning passed in a blur of uneventful classes and uninteresting conversation. I stole a glance at O'Malley as I was going from art to maths (and he from French to English, I made it my business to know his timetable). He was mesmerizing. all wavy hair and angular eyebrows, full lips and sharp jaw line. Then, mercifully, the bell went and break arrived, I took a breath and went to seal my destiny.

The school office was empty, as I knew it would be, the secretary went out for his morning cigarette everyday at 11:21 without fail. My window for opportunity was open and I was not going to miss it. I scanned the room searching for my choice of weapon, there it was shoved into the corner, covered in a thin layer of dust.

Eam had given me detailed instructions on how to work the intercom, his 6th Year failed prank preparations finally coming to some use. I recalled the steps I had memorized and flicked the red switch, turned the yellow dial up to three and began to speak. All students, teachers and staff were now tuned into my broadcast, I had everyone's undivided attention. Finally my moment had come.

"Student body", I began voice faltering with a combination of nerves and pure adrenalin. "I am a student like each and every one of you, a girl with the same emotions as you lot out there and like many of you all I have fallen in love. So Shane O'Malley, my soul mate, this one is for you with my dearest and most sincere love."

And off I went:

'My dear, my love, my Shane

What more in this life could I gain?

In your love I've been caught

You must get this a lot

But our love for eachother is plain

My dear, my love, my Shane

It's not like I'm going insane

I'm not playing tricks

But I need my next fix

For you are my brand of cocaine

My dear, my love, my Shane

You're so in control of my brain

And with every heart-beat

There's a love that's so sweet

Oh, my dear, my love, my Shane'

I left the office with my head held high and felt the weight of my suppressed love lifted from my weakened shoulders.My good mood was short lived as I was immediately sent to the Principal's office. But, who cared? I drifted there on a cloud full of love and a wisp of all things perfect.

So this was the minor set back in the world-wind romance. I was in the middle of the 'sad-scene'. You know what scene I am talking about. Where the hero and heroine are after breaking up (not in every case, obviously), usually due to a misunderstanding of epic proportions. The characters all sit in dramatic poses and the majority of the time it is raining. You can hear the softly ascending and descending of strings in the background. The girl usually cries, but cries in a pretty way where the tears fall gracefully down her cheeks. Not very realistic, when I cry my mascara smudges in horrific lines across my face, making me look like some eccentric singer in a Kiss tribute band, my eyes puff up like profiteroles and, well, you don't want the details of the snotty nose. Yet I was extremely comforted in the realization that the two lovers always end up together.

I sat there replaying the final scene of every romantic comedy on this good Earth, the two characters charge towards each other and collide in a passionate embrace, usually followed by an equally passionate kiss. The thought brought butterflies to my stomach, but, I had the chapstick ready to go.

It was fun picturing myself and O'Malley's first moments as a couple, I could not help but hear the strings building to a crescendo as we unite. I was interrupted mid-thought by my Principal who summoned me into the lion's den. There I was greeted with a truly horrendous sight.

My parents were pale with shock with deep looks of disappointment etched onto their faces. My brother looking guilty as hell but wildly entertained. Shane O'Malley looking both horrified and humiliated, definitely not flattered or joyous. They were all staring at me, each of them expecting some explanation for my, somewhat, odd behaviour. But Shane O'Malley still didn't love me, that stupid insignificant boy!

Sure he was beautiful, kind, creative (I am assuming on the last two), but he was obviously blind. How could he not see that I was a catch? So out I came with my final and most important poem.

'Alright, I'm done, I quit

I've been acting quite odd I admit

But this love got me goin'

And there was no way of knowin'

That with this love thing I'm deemed unfit

Alright, I'm done, I quit

I may have messed up a bit

But I wanted to share

How much I did care

But, good God, this love-stuff is bull—'

Watching Richard
Stephen Tol

Marie would not keep her mouth shut as we were doing the cliff walk in Dover. It had been a nice sunny day but big, dark, capacious, thundering rain clouds were coming in from France. The sun had gone down and it was getting dark. Richard was staying with my cousin Eileen. We were going to stay at Eileen's for the night and drive back to London the next day. Marie and I had been walking for almost three hours and my idea had not left my mind once. I had just told Marie my cynical idea. I was unsure if she would agree with me but it was for the best.

I told Marie that I wanted to take Richard back to Jamaica.

"He has just turned two, Marie, I think it would be better to move to Jamaica now and not in ten years! If we move in ten years, it will be difficult for Richard to say goodbye to his friends."

"London is not safe with the Great War, Marie. And Richard will not be able to handle the racism."

"You're acting stupid Michael; there is no war in London."

"Yeah, maybe not now but those Germans could invade at any time!"

"They will not invade our country, the British army is too strong for them!" she argued.

"We are not moving to that country! Their economy is outrageous! There is no way I am going to Jamaica. You can go if you want Michael, I'll find a new father for Richard. One that is not a foreign, drunken old man like you! One that can speak good English!"

"Do you want our son to be killed before he reaches twenty five because there's a high possibility of that happening, you know!" I warned her.

"You cannot choose what is right for our son! You have only been living here for ten years Michael!"

"At least I pay attention to the country's situation. I have never once seen you pick up a newspaper and finish it Marie. You're too obsessed with Catholicism. You go to church too much. You would probably understand Latin by now! You know what, I'm doubting God's existence. Why would he allow millions to die in a war?" I wondered.

Marie became furious with me. "God did not cause the war! It was people like you who did!" We were moving closer to the edge of the cliff. At this point, I was shaking in my boots. I was afraid of heights. I was extremely frightened.

"You can go back to Jamaica if you love your family so much because I'm not going with you. I'm keeping Richard; you're a bad influence on him."

Marie swung a punch at me but I caught her hand. It was awfully windy, pitch dark and nobody was around to help me. I slipped on some stones at the very edge of the cliff. I was barely back on my feet when I slipped again. I completely lost my footing. Marie grabbed my hand but she could not hold on.

My two feet slipped off the edge and were dangling in the air. I had grabbed onto a rock with my left hand. It was now pitch dark. Thunder and lightning struck. It began to lash rain. My hand was slipping from the rock. I panicked. I searched for something else to grab on to but there was nothing. My hand slipped and I began to fall. This was the end and I was only forty years old. I was floating. My life flashed before my eyes. Each raindrop carried a life memory. I had never experienced something that surreal before, not even in my wildest dreams. Blood rushed around my body.

I was falling for about ten seconds but it felt like ten minutes.

I hit the ground.

I was lying on a stony beach. I watched the rain lash down from the pitch dark sky. The thunder gradually became louder and I could see lighting striking over the horizon. Everything happened in the heat of the moment. I could not move, I was in shock. I lay there for about five minutes and thought about the whole argument. Maybe I was wrong to argue with Marie, maybe the idea of moving to Jamaica was wrong. I soon decided to stand up. I felt very strange, very light. Somehow, I did not feel any pain at all.

Marie must have gone back to Eileen's house to collect Richard and tell her about all that had just happened. It was a far walk to the town. I found it extremely difficult to find my way in the dark. The tide was coming in and hitting my feet. I had to run. I felt like I was in a nightmare. What was happening? I did not tire at all. I made it around the corner of the cliff in about forty minutes. I still was not tired. Something strange must have happened to me. I ran up the hill up onto the grass. I had run about eight-hundred metres and I was not even breathless. It took me another twenty minutes or so to reach Eileen's street. When I got there I spotted Marie straight away. I shouted her name but she didn't reply. When I caught up with her I tried to catch her attention again. She didn't answer, she kept walking. It was like I was invisible. We got to Eileen's house. Marie nervously walked down the driveway. She knocked on the door a few times before Eileen answered. "Marie, how dare you bang on my door like that? Where is Michael? Where is he? Give me some answers Marie!"

What was Eileen talking about? I was right there in front of her. Marie still hadn't answered Eileen's question. She was nervous, under pressure, it was so obvious.

"There has been an accident .Michael slipped off the cliff top." Eileen burst into tears. At this stage, I knew I was dead. It was the only reason for being painless, invisible and unheard. I was a ghost and I didn't know what to do. I must have been in hell because I was certainly not in heaven. I just wanted to tell them that I was there listening.

Marie stayed in Eileen's for the night with Richard.

There was nothing I could do to communicate with my son. What would I do as a ghost? Nobody could hear or see me. I could move through objects and follow people without them knowing. I felt that it was only right to follow Richard for the rest of his life. I wanted him to be safe from the likes of Marie.

But I didn't know how I would do this. Were there other ghosts around? Was I by myself? I didn't want to scare Richard as he was growing up. Should I have left him be? Did I have to be good to get to the other side? All of these questions bounced within me but there was no me. I was the only one who knew there was.

***

Richard had quite a difficult life. Marie never had a lot of money. She did do a good job on raising Richard considering all the problems he faced.

I watched over Richard when he found school hard, and when he was diagnosed with dyslexia at the age of 12. He tried his best though and that was all that mattered considering how talented he was in football. He began playing football when he was five. He had a natural talent. Scouts always noticed him but Marie would not allow him to join a club until he was ten. Richard ended up playing in Arsenal football club's youth academy. He was the star footballer on his team. He played as a forward and scored multiple goals which lead to winning leagues and cups. During all of Richard's football success, he still focused hard in school but his grades still did not improve. When Richard was fourteen, Marie decided to take him out of school as it wasn't helping him and it was costing too much money. Richard searched hard for work for over a year. Richard eventually got a job in 'Dickens's Bakery' when he was fifteen. Richard loved the bakery. It was right beside his football club and he could go there before and after football. It was the most popular bakery in London so it was busy every day which meant Richard earned more money. Richard loved his job and worked there until he was twenty two. The job made life easier for Marie and Richard.

Life was going great for Richard. He met a nice girl, Anne, he had a great job and he lived in a nice house. Throughout Richard's childhood, there were a lot of political changes in Europe. The Treaty of Versailles was passed in the year 1919. It caused a lot of controversy in Europe. Germany was greatly affected by this treaty. Germany was blamed completely for The Great War. Germany's military strength was hugely restricted and Germany lost a lot of land. Hitler's Germany invaded Poland on 1 September 1939. On 3 September, France and Britain declared war on Germany. Richard received a letter later that month that conscripted him to go to war on 20 September 1941 when Richard would be twenty three. The letter also stated that Richard had to train hard for the two years before he could leave. Richard's first impression was positive. He wanted to honor and represent his country and fight for his King just like the propaganda war posters encouraged him to. Richard's two years of training were positive. He married his lovely fiancée, Anne, a year before he went to war and he had his daughter, my granddaughter, Ava-Rose, ten months later. In the few months before war, Richard was full of emotion. Richard knew he was going to miss Anne and Ava but he also knew that he had to go to war. He was promised his job back at Dickens's for when he came back. However, it was going to be difficult to make the Arsenal team when he came back as there were plenty of great players in the academy who would be adults when Richard returned. Richard also seemed sad about not having me around for Ava. Richard started to think about the negative things that could happen to a soldier at war. The newspapers already had a lot of tragic stories in them; Richard certainly did not want to be one of them.

***

Two years later……

"Pass me the gun Richard, pass me the damn gun. Are you there Richard, wake up! Can you hear me?" Richard slowly began to open his eyes. He was unconscious. He had been hit in the head by a German soldier. His mate Jack was trying to wake him up. Richard finally woke up. He was lying against a wall in a field near Saxony, Germany.

Richard's division had been based in Germany for almost a year. They had previously joined with what was left of an American division.

Their objective was to back up some British spies, while investigating concentration and prisoner-of-war camps. The spies acted as Nazi generals. The spies had moved on ahead as Richard's division got stopped at the border of a camp.

There were three Nazi soldiers there guarding the camp's gates. One looked about thirty-five years of age while the other two were both young, tough-looking men with shaved heads. They were dressed with jet-black uniforms, big black boots, black police-like hats and red Nazi armbands. They quickly recognized that Richard's division were allies. Richard's division fired shots before the Germans could even reach for their guns. Jack dragged the dead bodies behind a tree on the left of the gates. Richard led the division to camp. It was about twenty meters away. Big grey walls surrounded it with barbed wire on top.

Richard didn't know what to expect. He felt sick thinking about what he might see. It was extremely difficult to run as it was lashing rain and the ground had turned muddy. Richard's feet were almost sinking in the mud. "Slow down, keep quiet" Richard whispered to his men as he spotted a sniper on lookout. They reached the tall, thick, grey walls. There was a gap in the walls which was separated by pillars. Richard took cover behind a pillar and he commanded the others to move to the other pillar. A German soldier spotted one of Richard's men as he left a cabin inside the walls. Richard shot him straight in the chest. The small man fell to the ground and blood gushed out of him. Richard commanded his men to run in and take cover. As Richard was running to hide behind a cabin, he was shot multiple times in his right leg by the sniper which he had spotted before. It was like a car had just driven right into him. Richard completely lost feeling in his leg and fell to the ground. He whacked his head off a concrete brick at the bottom of the cabin and lost consciousness. Jack ran over and commanded the others to keep fighting.

***

A month later……..

"Hello, hello. Where am I? Somebody help me!" Richard woke up in a hospital tent.

I was sitting right beside his bed. He hadn't yet noticed that his right leg had been amputated.

"You're okay son. Don't worry. I'm proud of you."

Richard panicked.

Contributors

Alicia Albu is sixteen, wary of morning people and easily amused when things rhyme. Bruises easily, hates it when cats don't respond to her meows. She insists on having the volume level on a multiple of 5. She likes carbohydrates, bears and gelato. Can't math. Aspires to one day have enough courage to ask for extra ketchup at McDonald's.

Laura Bourke is aged sixteen. She lives in Donabate with her parents, two brothers, and dog called Ruby. She is a lover of tea, swimming, music and ice-cream. She dislikes spiders, homophobes, hypocrites and attention seekers. She hopes to go into a career of nursing.

"If I had a world of my own everything would be nonsense."

Luke Collins is sixteen years old and is from Donabate, Co. Dublin. He likes going to the gym and going out with his friends. Art is his favourite subject in school. He has had a passion for art from a young age and wishes to pursue a career in it.

Matthew Dolan is sixteen and goes to Donabate Community College. He does taekwondo but is also training rigorously for a Netflix marathon. He especially likes rock but hates pop and dubstep.

Dylan Forde is sixteen years old, his birthday is 4th December. He is from Donabate, Co. Dublin. He enjoys going out with his friends, playing football and cycling. His favourite subject is history and he hopes to study it in college. He loves house music and is an excellent dancer.

Rebecca Kelly is sixteen years old and from Dublin. She enjoys watching cartoons, ranting about feminism on the internet and eating far too much chocolate. Her favourite band is the Red Hot Chili Peppers and she plans on marrying the lead singer. Her dream is to become a zoologist and live in a big house full of cats and various other cute animals.

Tom Knightly is a sixteen year old from Lusk, who currently resides in his parent's estate. Enjoys rugby and other sports. Loves bacon and cabbage or a good steak sandwich. Absolutely hates Supermac's and other cheesy fast food restaurant chains. Also not particularly fond of porridge.

Adam Lyons was born in Redcar, Middlesbrough, England in 1998. He loves rugby and eating pizza. He likes any music but Dubstep. Linkin Park is his favourite band. He hates heights and deep water. "I tried so hard and got so far but in the end it doesn't even matter".

Sadhbh Mac Lochlainn is a sixteen year old female. The only interesting thing about Sadhbh is her taste in music, which is most likely better than yours. She is very humble (probably more so than you).

Eoghan McGleenan was born in November 1997 and lives in Donabate, Co. Dublin. He is a student at Donabate Community College. He plays Gaelic Football for St. Patrick's GAA Club. He also enjoys surfing and kayaking. He received 10 A's in the Junior Certificate and likes playing video games.

Sarah Moore is a sixteen year old from Donabate. She likes listening to music and wasting her life online. She hates procrastinating and writing about herself. Her favourite food is pizza, she can't get enough of it. She wants to live in the city when she's older and study psychology.

Rachael Murray was born in August 1997. Her friends consider her tiny, she prefers fun sized. School bores her – she 'd prefer to be hanging out with friends or scrolling the internet for hours on end. Hates the colours yellow and orange - prefers purple and black. She has a big personality, but you won't see it unless she is comfortable around you.

Alex O'Dea is sixteen years old. She lives in Donabate. She has two younger sisters. She moved to California two years ago and moved back to Ireland last summer.

Adam O'Rourke loves to watch shows about geese. He also enjoys going on cycles with the lads and hitting the beach in the summer. He plays GAA for St.Pat's and soccer for St.Ita's. He loves it! Also enjoy a gaff party now and then.

Hazel O'Shea is the author of several (unfinished) works, which have been translated into no other languages and have been read by no one. She lives in Donabate with her family and various pets, and hates few things more than writing about herself in third person. She has really enjoyed the whole experience of writing for this anthology, but as to writing again, she may have to give it a couple of months.

Aaron Page is sixteen years old. He lives in Donabate. He plays half forward for St.Pat's in football and St.Ita's in soccer. He supports the greatest club in England, Manchester United.

Diane Pasague was born in the Philippines in 1997. She has lived in Dublin since she was four. Over time, she has developed a close relationship with watermelons, junk food and horror stories and she spends most of her time doing random things. Some of which include reading, listening to music and spending

long nights on tumblr or reading fanfiction. She is skilled in the areas of procrastination, multitasking and napping. She is also a typical Scorpio and no matter how much she denies it, she can be very judgemental and moody. She plans to study psychology, physics and philosophy.

Ghail Protacio was born in 1998 and is originally from the Philippines. She moved to Ireland at the age of four where she trained herself in the art of lip synching at the age of thirteen. She has since achieved honours such as successfully mouthing the lyrics to non-English songs. As well as being talented in useless areas,

she is also very generous, having adopted a number of stuffed animals during the course of her life. The latest addition was a family of homeless teddy bears that she officially took under her care last December. She dreams of peace, and of a world where one can roam side by side with dragons and unicorns. Vegetables are not her style.

Maeve Sweeney is sixteen and from Dublin. She lives in Donabate with her parents and older sister. She plays piano, is embarrassingly stubborn, has an addiction to P.G Wodehouse and has an irrational fear of birds.

Stephen Tol is 16 years old and was born in Volendam, the Netherlands in 1997 and raised in Dublin. He is currently in Transition Year in Donabate Community College. He lives with his Mam, his Dad, his brother, his two sisters and his two dogs. He eats cookies every day. He likes to play hockey for Portrane Hockey Club

Men's and under 16's teams and golf every week with his brother Killian. His friends call him Steve and he likes to go out as much as he can. He listens to Hip-hop, rap, RnB and pop music. His favourite music artist is the producer, singer-songwriter, rapper and pianist Richard Rawson.

Thank Yous

Fighting Words.

Sara Bennett, Deirdre Davys, Rosa Devine, Roddy Doyle, Helen Flanagan, Courtney Haley, Jean Hanney, Katie Healy, Maeve Healy, John Holohan, James Kirwan, Orla Lehane, Emmy Lugoye, Ray Lynn, Paul Murray, Emma Murtagh, Daragh O'Toole, Clara Phelan, Helen Seymour, Julie Steenson, Joan Torsney, Carol Walsh, Carissa Young.

Donabate Community College

Thank you to all the staff and dedicated volunteers at Fighting Words. We would like to thank Ms. Mary Lowry from the school's English Department who accompanied us every single Thursday to Fighting Words and also spent a generous amount of her free time assisting us with the task at hand and reaching our deadlines. Thanks also to our Principal, Mr. Anthony Creevey and Vice Principal, Mrs. Marian Flynn for their support. We would also like to thank our former Principal, Ms. Olive Laffoy. We are most grateful to our parents and families for their continuous support and encouragement. Finally thank you to all the students in our school who made contributions to various Fighting Words projects in the past. Without them, we may never have been given this opportunity.